Peaceful Farm Montessori School

Peggy E. Pate-Smith

Peaceful Farm Montessori School
Timely Tomes Publishing

Author: Peggy E. Pate-Smith
All rights reserved
http://peggyepatesmith.weebly.com

ISBN: 978-0-9826504-1-7
First Edition January 2014
Young Adult fiction

Summary: Peace, love, and middle school.
Miranda is in for the Heroic Journey of her life as
she stumbles her way through her first crush,
learning to make new friends, dealing with a tragic
accident, and finding a way to use her unique talents
to serve others.

Peaceful Farm Montessori School
By Peggy E. Pate-Smith

Every author is a dreamer taking what they know then spinning webs catching bits and pieces to create unchartered worlds to the delight of their readers. –p.e.p.s.

This book is dedicated to Dr. Betsy Coe, who used the teachings and philosophy of Dr. Maria Montessori in order to further the Montessori Middle School curriculum. Betsy, thank you for the difference you are making in the world.

Acknowledgements also go to Melinda Harris, principal of the Public Montessori School in Jackson, TN. Thank you for believing in the middle school and working so hard to make it a reality against all odds. Thank you for believing in me.

Thank you to Val McAvey, her husband Rich, and their kids for welcoming not only me but also my family into their home while I was doing my Montessori training. Your kindness will never be forgotten.

Special thanks to Sherry Arnold, for being the first one to read my stories and give me feedback. Thank you to Teri Thrasher for trusting me with her son as a student and making the choice to share all your artistic talents and grace with our classroom. Thanks to Bruce Green for literally being an answer to prayer and for your hard work and dedication to the students I love so much. Thanks to Jessica Donnell, who was not only a great editor but also a great encourager!

CHAPTER ONE...Miranda

"If people really wanted world peace as much as they all want a new television set, there would be world peace." ~John Lennon

Miranda had thick black hair and amazing green eyes, but everything else about her was so ordinary as to go unnoticed. She liked swimming, soccer and long conversations on the phone with her friends. She liked to paint her nails in wild colors to make up for the fact that she had to keep them very short in order to play her guitar.

She loved music, both old and new, and read books for fun, not just for school. Miranda lived in a white, two story house on the edge of a small town. Her room was miniscule but it had a big window that looked out over the town; the skylight over her bed gave her a winter view of Orion. She considered him a good buddy and liked the fact that he stood guard over her while she slept. Her room was painted sky blue. She had embellished the walls with butterflies, rainbows, quotes, and posters. It was her own little world and she loved it.

Her younger sister was a precocious nine year old named Sarah, but everyone called her Candy because she was so sweet natured. Her big brother, Matthew, was in college. He was sometimes moody, sometimes fun, so you never knew what to expect. He was the one who had taught her how to play the guitar. Matthew's band, "Green Eyed Boys" was popular both in the small town of Pete's Grove where Miranda lived, and at Mississippi State where he was majoring in art education.

Creativity ran through Miranda's family like water through a faucet. Her mother and father had met at a Renaissance fair where he had been a sword maker, and she sold beautiful medieval dresses and jewelry that she made herself. They had settled down when Matthew came along and now they ran a small private Montessori school on a farm south of town. The school name was "Peaceful Farm Montessori" often it was just referred to as "The Farm" because it had started out as a real farm.

Miranda's mother, Katura Cockrum, had inherited the farm when her Miranda's great grandfather, Abraham Winslow, had died. Long ago, it had been a dairy farm with a big garden and a grape orchard. Abraham's wife, Miranda's Great Grandmother, was named Tia, she had been a tiny woman about five feet, with not a bit of fat on her frame. Miranda's mother said Great Grandma Tia was so thin from keeping up with the farm. She had raised her own five children, and also took care of her sister's four children after her sister died during childbirth. Katura often said that Miranda had her Great Grandmother's beautiful smile. Miranda would often look at old pictures of the family and try to see the resemblance, but she guessed some things were never the same in pictures as they were in real life.

The farm had once been a huge operation, but the land had slowly been sold off as children grew up and moved away. The children chose to leave behind the hard work and a simple life in the country for a life of hard work and a hectic life in the city. The house, a huge barn, and about ten acres were all that remained. It was a great place for the tranquil atmosphere of a Montessori school.

Miranda had grown up at the school. She had been born when Matthew was on summer vacation from the first grade. When school started again in the fall, Miranda had slept snug in the baby sling draped around her mother's body like a new accessory in back-to-school clothing for teachers.

She had never known a world without pink towers or golden beads, and thought nothing of multiplying and dividing six digit numbers before she had finished kindergarten. The Montessori world had always been marvelous to her.

This year was different though. This year she was in the seventh grade and being the daughter of the school owners had both advantages and disadvantages. She loved the farm, but she couldn't help wondering what her life would have been like in a "regular school". She had friends at the local middle school, East Middle, and even though its big hallways intimidated her and sitting in desks all day listening to teachers prattle on seemed boring, she thought it would be exciting to eat lunch in a big, noisy, crowded cafeteria every day and be part of a school soccer team, not just the local Parks and Recreation team. Life was like that though, you could dream all you wanted, but you were stuck in the reality you woke up in.

I looked to the right of me; there was Susan Avery, my best friend. She was eating a hamburger and fries but talking about how awful it was to eat meat because it took so much grain and water to raise cattle just to be slaughtered for human food when there were so many humans dying of starvation because they didn't have clean water or enough food to eat. Just then Paul McCartney walked by singing, "All you need is love..." Suddenly the hamburger Susan had been eating hopped up and started dancing. Susan started jumping up and down, yelling, "See what I mean, people! All we need is just more love!" Then everyone in the cafeteria and all the hamburgers started singing and swaying while rattling their jewelry. I looked down at my milk carton and the girl on the face of the milk box started talking to me, "I think I have been kidnapped. I need to find my real family." I picked up the milk carton and took it to the school office and asked the school secretary to try to find the girl's family because I needed to go to math class. Then I tried to find the class but had no luck until five minutes before the school bell rang.

Miranda woke up to the sound of the phone ringing in her ear. Charlie was calling to see if she could get a ride to school. Her mom had been called into work early, there had been a bad wreck and she was needed at the hospital. Charlie Townsend was Miranda's best friend at The Farm. They had been friends since the third grade when Charlie had first come to the school.

Charlie hadn't spoken at all for the first three weeks. Katura had told Miranda that Charlie was upset and needed time to recover from a bad experience. What really happened was that Charlie's dad had been driving too fast with Charlie in the back seat on a dark country road and lost control of his car. The car had flipped several times and her dad had gone through the front windshield. Charlie had been buckled in the back seat. When the car finally stopped she was o.k. but very bruised up. She had crawled out to find her father dead on the side of the road. She stayed with her dad until a young couple on their way to church the next morning passed by and found her. Shortly after that Charlie and her mother, Linda, moved back to Pete's Grove to live with Charlie's grandparents, Leon and Martha Coffee. Charlie's mom was a nurse in the local emergency room.

"Of course Charlie, let me tell my mom. We will probably be there about 7:30." Miranda put the phone back on the hook and snuggled back under her bright pink and purple comforter.

She would have to wake up for real in a few minutes but waking up slowly was a good thing to her. School didn't start until 8:30, but they always got there early to make sure everything was set up and ready to go. "Preparing the environment" was what her mom called it. Miranda usually used that time to practice her guitar. The little kids that arrived early liked to listen to her play. They were usually pretty sweet, except for Jeffrey, he was in the fourth grade and when Miranda complained about what a brat he was, her father would always say, "Some people just need more love and understanding than others."

Her dad was kind like that, Miranda still thought Jeffrey was a just a brat though.

Miranda's father, Peter Cockrum, was a tall man, with bright red hair, a full beard, and a booming laugh that could be heard all the way through the school house. While her mother tended to the business side of the school and occasionally taught in the lower elementary classrooms, her father took care of the house itself, the barn, the yard, the animals, as well as monitored the older students at times. Miranda had to admit her parents were pretty amazing.

Her mother had majored in education, getting her degree from the University of Texas, and her dad had studied art and political science, dropping in and out of college until he finally dropped out to join the Renaissance fair circuit where he had met her mom. She had been doing the circuit for a short break after college. Her dad said that he was reading a book under a tree on one of his breaks when she walked past him. He said she smelled of apples and flowers and he fell in love with the way she smelled even before he looked up and saw the dark haired angel whose eyes were as deep green as the ocean. Those green eyes and her delicious scent changed his life forever.

Miranda loved that story. She knew a lot of kids whose parents were divorced and so she knew it was special to have parents that were not only still together but also still loved each other very deeply. She hoped she would someday marry someone that looked into her eyes the way her dad looked at her mother.

Miranda swung her feet off the bed and breathed in the cool morning air. She was looking forward to Halloween in a few weeks for several reasons, but one of them was that right after Halloween it would be daylight savings time and she wouldn't have to struggle so hard to wake up while it was still dark. Miranda did not consider herself a morning person, but then again, what self-respecting teenager would? She looked at the Tinkerbellee alarm clock next to her bed. The neon green numbers flashed 6:45.

Miranda took a few minutes to stretch before climbing down the stairs to the big bathroom where she could take a shower. She could hear her mom singing in the kitchen. The smell of eggs and veggie bacon tickled her nose. Yum!

After a quick shower, Miranda pulled blue jeans and her favorite yellow sweater out of the closet. She had bought it at the local Goodwill with her birthday money. It was so soft! Miranda liked soft stuff of any kind.

"Good Morning Mom" Miranda whispered as she took her seat in front of the plate of eggs and veggie bacon strips laid out in front for her.

"Hey sweetie. Who called early this morning?"

Whoops. She had almost forgotten.

"That was Charlie, and she needs a ride to school. There was an accident and Ms. Linda had to go into work early."

"Hmm…O.K. We need to step up the pace then. Candy, are you ready to go?"

Candy finished off the tall glass of orange juice in front of her. "Yep."

Miranda looked at her little sister; she was wearing a pair of pink tights, an orange dress and a purple hair bow woven into her curly auburn hair. A wild look, but on Candy the ensemble looked perfectly normal. Only Candy could pull together such crazy colors and still look absolutely precious.

Miranda gulped down the rest of her breakfast and went to grab her book bag. She was glad she had put everything ready to go the night before. She made her way to their little Prius parked outside the sunroom door. The shiny red car gleamed in the early morning sunlight, a few fall leaves decorating the front of the hood. Miranda dumped her book bag in the floor of the front seat and jumped in, carefully buckling her seat belt before flipping down the mirror to check her hair. Passable.

Candy slid into the back seat. "Did Charlie know who was in the accident?"

"I don't know, she didn't say."

Miranda's dad was holding the back door open for Katura to come through. They kissed goodbye as her mom juggled the books, laptop computer, and a cobalt blue mug filled with coffee. It was one of their rituals; they never left each other without a kiss goodbye, even if they knew they would see each other again in a few minutes. When her mom got to the car she handed Candy all her stuff and took a sip from the still steaming coffee before calmly entering the car. Her mom was like that. A tornado could be whipping around the house and she would still be calm and smiling.

The little red Prius pulled up in front of a tiny yellow house with a black mailbox that had "Coffee and 352 Maple St." stenciled on it in neat white letters. Charlie was waiting on the white swing on the front porch. She slowly got her stuff together and joined them at the car. Gingerly she added her own book bag to the growing pile of stuff in the back seat next to Candy.

"Thanks for the ride Mrs. Cockrum."

"You are more than welcome Charlie. How are you this morning?"

"I'm fine, just sleepy. Mom woke me up early because she had to leave and she didn't want me to oversleep."

Miranda turned in her seat so she could have a better view of her tiny, blonde hair, blue eyed friend. "Have you heard any details about what happened?"

"Mom said it was a car accident. A girl was texting on her phone and pulled out in front of a family on vacation. The girl had missed a stop sign so she was going pretty fast."

Katura sighed, "That is scary, and sad. Do you know who the girl was?"

"Emily Hunter."

The name sounded familiar to Miranda but she couldn't quite place it. Charlie continued on, "She is a senior at the high school; mom said she was on her way to an early job and was late for work. She works at the Bluebird Café preparing for the breakfast crowd before school starts."

Candy readjusted the books beside her and then said, "Do you know if anyone was hurt?"

"No, mom just said it was pretty bad. She didn't have time to tell me much else. She just called to make sure I hadn't gone back to bed. I hadn't though because I needed to finish up on the guiding question essay for language. Did you get yours finished Miranda?"

Miranda looked at her friend and grinned, "Mostly." She had actually been up late finishing it and needed to go back and edit it one last time. Miranda was a good student but she didn't like to brag so she usually avoided straight answers about how quickly she got things done. Last night had been the exception though, it was the end of the first cycle of the year and the essay was a summary of the guiding questions of what they had studied in language during that six week cycle. The theme for the cycle was Forces. So Miranda had been thinking about the forces that shape good writing. She had found it difficult to express all that she had learned.

Writing and language were turning out to be more challenging for her than math. She loved math. She loved the way things came to neat conclusions in math. In literature she had already realized that problems are not always easily solved. Her teacher, Miss Walker, had a way of introducing stories that weren't always easy to deal with and made her think deeper about things than she had ever thought about. Miss Walker talked about "social justice" a lot. Montessori schools are big on talking about peace, but Miss Walker felt there would never be peace in the world until there was social justice, and social justice would never occur until people stepped out of their comfort zones. The stories they had been reading in class were all about stepping out of comfort zones. Before this year she had never thought very much about prejudice, or homelessness, or how lonely people could be. The stories they read made all those things more real in her mind. They were hard things to think about but it made her feel good that Miss Walker felt like they were mature enough to tackle big subjects.

One of the things they did in their class that Miranda loved the most was "Socratic dialogue". It was something they did to discuss literature, but also to observe how they discussed literature. They broke the class up into two groups. One group formed an inner circle that discussed the text. The other group formed a big circle around the smaller inner circle. The outer circle just listened to the discussion and took notes on how the inner group talked to one another so they could give feedback. The feedback would help the people in the inner circle know if they needed to speak up more or not talk over each other and stuff like that.

It was fun and Miranda felt like she had learned a lot during the process. The first time she was in the inner circle the text was talking about a homeless man. It was interesting, not just reading the text but getting to share what she had thought about it, and hearing what other people thought about it. Socratic dialogue was different because it was just the students discussing it, not like the younger classrooms where a teacher asked you questions about the story and you only got to answer one or two questions. Discussing the stories in this way made her feel like her opinion really mattered. It was also interesting to discuss big ideas with her peers.

The Prius pulled into the driveway of the Peaceful Farm Montessori School. Katura guided the car into her special parking space next to the big green barn. The barn had been transformed into classroom space for two classes of nine to twelve year olds and one big class of middle school students. The middle school class had twenty students and most of them had been at the farm for many years. The two six to nine year old classes met in the farm house. Katura's office was also in the farm house. She headed that direction and then reminded the girls to check on the animals before they went to the barn.

Miranda, Charlie, and Candy ambled over to the common area of the farm. Here there were some chickens, some rabbits, and a few turtles. The girls checked the water for the animals and gave them extra food. Miranda liked taking care of the animals. It made her feel responsible. She didn't have any pets at home because Matthew had allergies, but here at the farm they had always had several different kinds of animals. Her favorite had been the peacocks. They were so beautiful when they spread out their feathers. That's sort of how she felt now, like being in middle school was a time for her to spread out her feathers and show what she was made of. She missed the peacocks and hoped her dad would get more someday.

The animals came to the farm in various ways. Some were animals that just needed a home, the peacocks had been that way. They came from a farm down the road that had too many and donated some to the farm. Unfortunately the farmer and his wife had moved away to be closer to their grown up kids who lived in Nashville. Their farm stood empty, no one had come in to buy it, and there were no more new broods of peacocks or any other kind of animal. Miranda hated driving past the empty farm, it made her feel sad and she missed the animals.

Miranda looked at Candy. She had Midnight, the dwarf bunny, and was petting its soft black fur. The combination of Candy's wild outfit and the black bunny looked so good together that Miranda wished she had a camera. Miranda liked to take pictures and was the "unofficial" photographer for the school. Some of her pictures had even won awards at the local fair. Her favorite had been a picture of Candy when she had been about 5 years old. Candy had been in blue jean overalls, with a big blue bow in her red hair and she was picking red tulips from the flower bed in front of the school.

Her mom had not been pleased that she had encouraged Candy to pick the tulips but was happy for Miranda that she had won first place in the youth photography division of the fair that year. She said it almost made up for the tulips being trampled and plucked up in the prime of their life.

The animals had been fed, watered, loved on, and seemed content so the girls moved inside the barn. The barn had a big center section that was referred to as "the commons". The commons had an area with couches and wooden coffee tables. There were large plants and a big window that flooded the room with light. The white walls had seven quilts hanging on them. It was traditional for each of the eighth grade classes to make a quilt that represented themselves and their time at the school before they moved on to high school. Miranda's brother Matthew had put a guitar and a paint brush on his quilt block. Matthew not only played guitar but also wrote his own music. His class had made the first quilt. She liked to sit under it because it made her feel close to him. She hoped some of his talent would drip down from the quilt onto her if she sat under it long enough. She especially hoped this when she was working on something like the essay.

Miranda looked back over the essay, she checked to see if she had answered both of the guiding questions and followed the format of an essay that Miss Walker had carefully gone over with them. Her introduction paragraph should be in the form of a narrative, have a topic sentence, three reasons that backed up the topic sentence, a final sentence that expressed how she felt about the topic. Then she had a paragraph for each of the three reasons. Her conclusion paragraph restated her topic, gave the three reasons again and had a final sentence with a future thought about the topic. She checked for correct spelling, punctuation and made sure she had indented each paragraph.

She felt pretty good about it. She asked Candy to listen as she read it aloud to her. Miss

Walker always said that reading aloud would help you catch errors and help you check for ease of reading that you couldn't always get when you just read your own writing to yourself. Miranda made a few changes then walked over to the nearest computer. She put in her jump drive and pulled her paper up on the screen to make the changes and then clicked the printer icon.

She was exiting out of the program when Josiah walked in. Miranda looked at the tall eighth grade boy. His lean frame made him look like he was mostly arms and legs but Miranda didn't care, he was still the cutest boy in the school. She always tried to be calm around him but always walked away feeling like she had just put her size eight Converse into her mouth.

Miranda smiled a big smile, "Hi Josiah".

"Oh, um, hi Miranda." He seemed distracted. Miranda wondered whether she should ask why or let him have time alone. As she was trying to decide, she heard the farm bell ring outside. Students started piling into the barn. Miranda walked to her locker. The lockers were special because only the middle school students had them. They were made of wood and the first ones had been made by Matthew's class, more had been made as the school had grown from that original class of nine students.

When she was little Matthew would keep yogurt balls in a glass jar in his locker and would give her one every day after school. She had decided to continue the tradition and kept a supply on hand for Candy. Miranda stored her books and got ready for community meeting.

Community meeting was probably Miranda's favorite part of the day. All twenty of the middle school students would sit together on the couches and chairs in the commons. They would start the meeting by doing something called, "PACE". It was a series of physical exercises that involved moving your right hand across the midline of the body to the left side and your left hand over to the right side. Miss Walker told them the purpose of it was to help the right and the left side of the brain work together so they would be more effective learners. Miranda picked up her blue water bottle with "Peaceful Farm Montessori School" written on the side and took a big swig of water. Just as she did Stephanie Westwood crossed her eyes and made her laugh. Just her luck, Josiah was passing by at that moment and was the target of her impromptu water burst.

"Oh my goodness, Josiah, I am so sorry." She gushed as she felt her face turning bright red.

Josiah just shrugged as he wiped some moisture off his cheeks. He kept walking. Why couldn't the floor just open up and swallow her?

Miranda snapped the lid on the bottle and put it at her feet. She looked up in time to see Stephanie's smirk of braces. Stephanie was also in the eighth grade, with an outgoing personality she could always make you laugh, but sometimes you weren't sure if she was laughing with you or at you. At this moment Miranda was pretty sure she was being laughed at.

After PACE was something called, "Center". That was when the pile of left over belongings that had been piled on the center coffee table was claimed by the various students that had accidentally left them laying out the day before. The stack of notebooks, textbooks, and pens usually belonged to the same two or three people which made Miranda wonder just how "accidental" their leaving behind their belongings actually was. Sure enough T.J. collected his binder and his current novel. Greg claimed his binder and his five subject notebook and Toby claimed a poster he had been working on with his version of a creation story. A few loose papers were claimed, but luckily nothing of hers had been left behind.

Charlie's group was leading the community meeting. The middle school had twenty students but was divided up into smaller groups called, "color groups". The color groups had four students each. Charlie's group was the chocolate group and consisted of a short seventh grade girl named Amy, who was new to the school that year, Toby, also a seventh grader, and an eighth grade boy named Malcolm. Malcolm and Charlie were taking turns reading out Trivial Pursuit cards to quiz the students. They called this part of the community meeting, "Challenge" and the purpose was to wake up their brains and get them thinking.

Miss Walker had told them the teenage brain worked a little different from humans of other ages and their circadian rhythms caused them to be a little off from the rest of the world. She said that was why they had a harder time going to sleep at night and a harder time waking up in the morning.

Diana Turner answered the last question. The question was about the name of the hotel where the Watergate scandal had taken place. The answer was easy if you knew it, but Miranda hadn't been called on. Diana was in the eighth grade; she had a straight A average and would rather spend her Saturdays at the library rather than the mall. Miranda figured Diana would grow up to be the president of Harvard or something.

The next part of the meeting was acknowledgements. This was a time when people could publically say thank you for something a classmate had done for them. Charlie acknowledged Miranda for giving her a ride to school that morning. Steven acknowledged Diana for helping him understand the math assignment from the night before, and Ling May acknowledged Christopher for helping her carry in her project.

After acknowledgements there was a time for sharing. This was the highlight of the community meeting for Miranda. During sharing you could share anything going on in your life. Sometimes this part took a long time because several students usually shared and sometimes they would forget the one sharing per person guideline.

Amy's brown ponytail swung from side to side as she looked around the room before announcing, "Does anyone have anything to share?"

Brent's muscular arm shot up first. Amy called on him. "My soccer team won on Saturday and I didn't have to play goalie so that was great."

"Ling May" Amy continued.

"I have a part in the Nutcracker ballet; I'm going to be a soldier. I am really excited about it even if it means I will have to practice a lot between now and December."

Miranda shot a look at Ling May's brother, Jon. The dark haired boy was smiling. Miranda could tell he was proud of his little sister.

"Kelton." Amy said as she called on the large, grinning eighth grader sitting next to Miranda.

"Christopher came over to my house Saturday and we made up a cool new game kind of like a mix between chess and cards. We call it "chards". Christopher and I can teach anyone that would like to play with us."

The meeting went on with different people sharing. Miranda was paying more attention to Josiah though. He didn't really seem very interested in the meeting as he distractedly raked his hand through his shaggy blond hair. She wondered again if something was bothering him.

"Observer."

Toby looked down at the orange folder on his lap. The observer's job was to watch how people behaved during the meeting and remind people after the meeting was over if they hadn't been following the guidelines set up by the community early in the year as appropriate behavior for community meetings.

Appropriate behavior was a phrase that applied anytime a student forgot themselves and acted rudely. Miranda got tired of hearing it sometimes but she could appreciate the meaning of it. One thing she loved about the Farm was that most of the time the students were respectful. They were respectful not because they were afraid of being punished but rather because they all seemed to realize that things just seemed to go smoother when they all worked together, and at least tried to be respectful. Her mother often said, "Students don't usually need to be punished, they just need to be taught and re-taught if they make poor choices. Most students are not bad. They just forget themselves and what is expected of them. They need to be gently reminded."

Miranda was glad that her parents had that kind of attitude. When she got in trouble her parents would sit down and talk with her about the choices she had made and discuss how to make better choices in the future. Usually she only got a consequence if she messed up in the same way twice. Once she forgot to take out the trash on trash day two weeks in a row. As a consequence her dad made her ride in his beat up old pickup truck through town to take the trash to the city dump, and she had to walk around her neighborhood with a plastic bag and pick up all the trash on her block. Ugh! She never forgot after that. She recognized the connection and it helped her make wiser decisions in the future: every Wednesday on her calendar now had a big red T on it as a reminder to take out the trash.

For the most part Miranda felt like her parents were fair. Her friend Susan's parents seemed to ground her all the time for the silliest things, and secretly Miranda suspected that most of the time Susan's parents found things to be upset about when they needed a babysitter for Susan's little brother, Stewart.

Toby was finishing up his observer's notes when Miranda's father walked in the door. Miss Walker stood up to confer with him for a few minutes then turned back to the class. Miranda loved the way Miss Walker's dark skin always made her smile seem so bright.

"Ladies and Gentlemen, this morning we are going outside to work in the garden with Mr. Cockrum for a while. Steven, could you please get the gloves for us? Hannah and Caroline please get the watering cans and fill them up."

Miranda watched the two thin girls hop up and immediately start giggling. Caroline's ivory skin in perfect contrast to Hannah's ebony complexion and their constant companionship always made Miranda think of piano keys playing a lively tune. Sometimes Miranda wondered if they giggled in their sleep, conjuring up common dreams to giggle about together.

The rest of the students got up and started walking behind Mr. Cockrum. Miranda waited for Charlie.

"Does Josiah seem unusually quiet to you?" Miranda whispered.

"I hadn't really noticed it, but now that I think of it, maybe so. I wonder what is wrong."

"Do you think it is because I accidentally spit on him this morning?" Miranda said, recalling her earlier embarrassing moment.

"I don't think so Miranda, although it was kind of gross and really funny." Charlie joked.

"Thanks for the support pal." Miranda said as she playfully poked her.

When they got out into the garden most of the class had already been given assignments. They claimed their gloves from Steven and started towards the compost bin. Their job was to empty the compost from the bin into a wheel barrow, then take the compost to the raised garden bed where new plants were about to be planted. Charlie and Miranda scooped out the compost then Miranda started pushing the wheelbarrow to the new bed. Miranda turned to ask Charlie if she wanted to spend the night at her house on Friday when she felt a wobble of the front wheel and heard Charlie say, "Watch out for that…" but it was too late. Miranda's feet got tangled in the green hose T.J. had left lying in the grass. Down went Miranda, down went the wheel barrow, and over went the compost, all over…Josiah.

CHAPTER TWO...Strawberry Fields

Miranda stared up into the night sky. Her mom sometimes said, "The nice thing about life is that it only happens one day at a time, and tomorrow is a new day." Miranda had gone to bed early hoping her dreams would erase the image of Josiah covered in compost and her not so graceful face plant in the grass.

I noticed it was getting darker; the forest path I was walking on seemed to be getting smaller. The trees were denser here and I started walking faster. Why had I come in here and how was I going to get out? Everything around seemed unfamiliar. Suddenly it started raining and the rain was turning into a thunderstorm. Crack. Crack. Boom! The trees behind me were falling, covering the path. Now there was no way that I could turn around and leave the forest the way I came in. I would have to go forward. I started running but when I did I noticed something green following close behind me. Oh no! It was a snake. I had to get out of there quickly, the snake was getting closer. It was just about to trip me and eat me alive. I needed to do something quickly. Then I remembered that I had a flashlight with me. I turned it on and could see the path ahead a little easier. I started running faster.

The faster I ran the further behind the snake seemed to be and before I knew it I was in a big clearing. It was a big strawberry field. There was Charlie, Malcolm, and Stephanie. They were all there, the entire Peaceful Farm middle school class, working away in the strawberry field. Josiah was walking towards me; his sandy blonde hair brushing the collar of his white Peaceful Farm t-shirt. The bright white of the t-shirt contrasted with his tan arms. He handed me a strawberry and said, "Are you o.k. Miranda? You look a little freaked out." I looked into his huge brown eyes and mumbled, "I'm fine. Everything is o.k."

It seemed like my whole class was staring at me, but then they all smiled and went back to work singing, "Strawberry Fields Forever".

Miranda hit the snooze button on her alarm clock and snuggled back under the covers.

CHAPTER THREE...Life, Laughter, Love

The middle school year was comprised of six cycles. The first cycle was an orientation cycle and only a few weeks long. It was all about getting to know each other and doing team building activities while figuring out the expectations for school work. After that introduction cycle there were five more cycles, each lasting six weeks. The first four weeks were very intensive study cycles, then a week of testing and finishing up work, and then came the immersion cycle. This was the best part of the middle school curriculum, the part her friend Susan at East Middle was the most jealous of. This was an entire week of doing something unique and fun.

Each of the cycles had a different theme, the first full length cycle for year B was Forces, and then came Structures, Power, Changes, and the last cycle of the year would be Balance. The curriculum had an A year and a B year. Next year would be the A year and its themes were different. This allowed them the chance to spread out the entire curriculum that needed to be taught in both 7th and 8th grade.

Students at Peaceful Farm took the state standardized test so they needed to be prepared but they didn't stress out about it the way Susan had told her the teachers seemed to stress out in traditional schools. This was another reason Susan was jealous. Katura had a strong belief that the quality of students The Farm produced could be told in their lives much clearer than a test score could ever predict. Her relaxed attitude helped both the teachers and the students at The Farm to be calm about the test when they took it. Test scores had always been high, so the strategy must have worked on some level.

To keep with the theme of the cycle, in a few days the class was spending a week at a special training center meant to train people to go into developing third world countries. They would be learning about the forces that were keeping people in high poverty areas from getting ahead and learn simple ways of using supplies that those people would have on hand to help improve their lives. Miss Walker had told them it was also about learning how education can be a powerful force to bring more social justice into the world. The middle school would be helping with some of the projects the training center was implementing. Miranda could hardly wait to go! It was going to be so much fun.

Miranda and Charlie were sitting on the brass bed in Charlie's room discussing the trip when the phone rang. Charlie jumped up and grabbed it, not that she had to jump up, her grandparents rarely answered the phone having gotten use to having a teenager in the house always eager to answer it for them. Miranda sipped her hot chocolate. It was her third cup. Charlie's grandmother made amazing hot chocolate and Miranda took full advantage of her generosity.

Charlie returned to the room with a big grin on her face. "My mom is on the phone, she is at the grocery store getting stuff for dinner. She wants to know what time you have to be home tonight."

"By six, if she can take me by then, if not I can call my mom to pick me up."

Charlie relayed the news to her mom and came back into the room.

"She will be here in a few minutes. She said we have time to stop by the hospital and see Mrs. Love's new baby!" Mrs. Love had been the fine arts teacher at the school and had fallen in love with the U.P.S. driver that delivered packages to the school. They had gotten married at Peaceful Farm last fall. Mrs. Love hadn't returned to school this year because she was expecting a baby.

"Oh! How exciting! Did she have a boy or a girl?"

"It was a girl."

"That's cool. Candy will be excited, she was betting on a girl."

Miranda had thought it was unique that the Loves had not wanted to know whether or not it was a boy or girl until the baby made its appearance. Mrs. Love had said she liked surprises and you didn't get as many when you were a grown up.

Miranda and Charlie felt important walking with Ms. Linda through the hospital. She had let the girls know that they couldn't stay long because Mrs. Love needed her rest, but Mrs. Love had given her permission for the girls to visit because she was excited to show off her new baby to two of her favorite former students. The maternity ward had lots of blue and pink balloons everywhere. They stopped in front of a door with a big pink Mylar balloon that declared, "It's A Girl!"

Mrs. Love and her husband were beaming at their newborn daughter when the girls walked in.

"She is so cute!" Charlie exclaimed. The rosy cheeked infant was practically bald except for a very fine dusting of blonde fuzz on the top of her head. She was wearing a brown outfit that had pink writing that said, "Important things can come in small packages." The girls read the shirt and then looked at Mr. Love and giggled.

Miranda was the first to ask, "What did you name her?"

"Zoe Gelasia Love"

"Zoe is a Greek word for life isn't it…hmm." Her eyes lit up in recognition of the quote that Mrs. Love had on the bumper sticker of her little red VW bug.

"So I'm guessing that Gelasia means laughter." She exclaimed with delight.

"That is right! You have been studying your etymologies. It is also Greek, and you guessed correctly. Her name means, "Life, Laughter, Love.""

The girls spent a few minutes catching up with Mrs. Love about things going on at the school and then gave her a hug and said good bye. They were almost to the car when Miranda realized how badly she needed to go to the bathroom. It must have been all the yummy hot chocolate that she drank. At the exact same time Charlie realized that she had left her camera in Mrs. Love's room. They agreed to go their separate ways and meet back at the car so they could get Miranda home by six.

Miranda hurried down the hall to find the bathroom. She was a little turned around because the hospital had been doing a lot of remodeling and things seemed a lot different from the last time she had been there. Finally she saw an arrow that pointed to the restrooms. She started to push the door open when it seemed to open quickly on its own. She hurried forward and ran smack into the person coming out of the restroom. Only it wasn't just any person. It was a boy. A tall, lanky, tan, sandy blonde, brown eyed boy. It was Josiah.

Miranda was so confused. What was Josiah doing coming out of the girl's restroom? That was when she looked at the sign on the door a little closer. It wasn't the girls' restroom he was trying to come out of. It was the boys' restroom she was trying to go in to.

Miranda turned bright red. "Oh, my goodness. I am so sorry Josiah. I read the sign wrong. I really had to go to the bathroom and in my hurry I thought this was the right one." Great, now he was not only going to think she was a klutz but she was also stupid.

Blink and breathe before saying anything else. That was one of the frontal lobe strategies Miss Walker had been trying to teach them for when they got into difficult situations...and this was definitely in that category!

"That's o.k. Miranda, the new construction is confusing. The girls' restrooms are around the corner."

Josiah was like that. Kind even when he had a perfect right to hate her for all the stupid klutzy things she did around him. He could have made fun of her and made her feel even more stupid, but that wasn't Josiah. He was just kind, and that made Miranda like him even more.

"Oh, o.k., thanks. By the way, I'm here with Charlie, we just came by to see Mrs. Love's new baby girl. Is that why you are here?" She wasn't trying to be nosy, she just wanted to change the subject away from her directional impairment, but as soon as she asked she looked at Josiah's face and wished she hadn't said anything, he looked so sad.

"No. My step sister, Emily, was in a bad car wreck and she is here."

"That is awful, I'm so sorry." Miranda gasped.

Josiah's voice began to falter, "She is in a coma. The wreck was her fault. She was in a hurry on her way to work. She hit a family in a jeep. They are all o.k. which is great, but Emily is not doing so well."

The car accident that Ms. Linda had gone into work early for. Emily Hunter was Josiah's step sister, which was why the name had sounded so familiar.

"Josiah, I'm so sorry. Is there anything we can do?" Miranda reached out and touched his arm without thinking.

"No, not really, we are just waiting. In fact I better go; my mom is supposed to pick me up in a few minutes."

"Well, I will be thinking about Emily, and about your family. Let me know if there is anything you need."

"Thanks."

She smiled at him and he smiled back. It was one of those moments when life seems to open some kind of magic portal and you know for sure that you have just done something positive. For once she walked away from Josiah not feeling awkward, sad for him, but for once not awkward.

At least the mystery of why Josiah had been distracted had been solved. Miranda thought about Emily as she walked to the car to meet Charlie and Ms. Linda. Life always seemed to be throwing curve balls at you. Good and bad, happiness and sadness, it was always a continuous cycle. When she got to the car she told Charlie and Ms. Linda about running into Josiah…literally.

Charlie laughed, "Good grief Miranda, you poor thing. You are like a magnet of disaster any time that boy is around you."

"I know." Miranda agreed morosely. "It is like I am fated to make a fool out of myself every time he gets near. Actually I was glad to see him this time though. I found out why he has been so sad. Emily Hunter, the high school girl that was in the car accident, is Josiah's step sister."

Ms. Linda adjusted the car mirror and looked back at them. Her look told them that Emily was not doing well. Miranda sighed, "I wonder why he didn't say anything at school."

Charlie got very quiet then slowly responded, "Sometimes when something hurts really badly it is hard to find words for the pain."

Miranda looked at Charlie, if anyone knew the truth of that statement, it would be Charlie. Charlie looked out the window as Miranda reached over and squeezed her hand.

CHAPTER FOUR...Helping Hearts and Hands

"Prayer through action." Miranda read the neatly lettered sign on the wall of the Helping Hearts and Hands training center wall. The class had gathered in the dining hall to get their assignments for the morning.

The man at the front had shaggy brown hair and a faded Auburn University sweat shirt on. He was talking to the students about various projects going on at Hearts and Hands. One project had to do with ways to help people in third world countries drill for clean water. Miranda already knew that clean water was an issue because Peaceful Farm held fundraisers each year on World Water Day, March 22, to raise money for the Amman Imman water project in the Azawak valley in Africa. This project was started by a woman who was a former Montessori student. The people in that region had to walk for many miles for water and dig very deeply, but still there was not enough water, or the water was too muddy. The Amman Imman project was helping the people to boredrill very deeply so they could get fresh clean water. The project's name meant, "Water is life. Milk is hope."

Miranda had always been touched by how critical this issue was; it fit right in with Miss Walker's thoughts about peace and social justice. If people didn't have their basic needs met, how could they even begin to think about peace, and how could people who did have their daily needs met refuse to reach out and help?

Miss Walker was adamant that the world was one planet and we needed to see people in other parts of the world as friends we just hadn't met yet. She said it was similar to how we didn't always get along with the people in our class. We were also not always going to understand or get along with people in other parts of the world, but blowing up our classroom wasn't the answer and blowing up other parts of our planet made no sense either. She said that the things done to help others would always eventually help us in one way or another. It made Miranda think about that old Aesop's tale of the mouse chewing the lion out of the rope trap.

Twenty percent of the world's population uses up fifty eight percent of the world's resources. America was a wealthy country and often guilty of using up more than it needed. Miranda suspected it was more because of being unaware than greed, but it seemed reasonable to her that America might someday be the lion caught in a trap and need that mouse for help. Not that people should be helped just in case we need their help someday, but it just made sense to her to think about the ramifications of actions, good or bad. "Think globally, act locally" was another sign Miranda had read on the center's wall.

Miranda listened to faded sweat shirt man talk about the simple drills being made that would help in areas where water was scarce, but perhaps not as scarce as in the Azawak valley.

He went on to talk about the clay tiles they would also be making this week and how beneficial these were for families who needed floors for their homes so they were not walking in mud when the rainy seasons hit.

The main project for the week was going to be working on a straw bale house. The house was going to be used as a dormitory for students when they came to Hearts and Hands so they didn't have to camp out. Miranda was excited about this even if she liked camping out. Miranda had seen the straw house on the drive into the training center. Bales of straw stacked up like the paper brick walls she once played with as a kid. She wondered if the Three Little Pigs had ever thought of building their house like that. Perhaps they would have been less afraid of the big bad wolf if they had. The straw house was almost finished and the Peaceful Farm students were going to help with plastering the walls. The chocolate, red, and yellow groups were going to be working on the outside of the house while the blue and green groups were working on the inside of the house.

Miranda and Charlie got up and followed the groups down the walking path to the straw house. Miranda thought about her group, the red group, which consisted of Kelton, Ling May, and Christopher. It had been a good group to work with, even if Kelton and Christopher had been more interested in talking about video games than working on projects. Kelton and Christopher had shared the leadership since they were both 8th graders, but sometimes Miranda had felt like she and Ling May spent large amounts of time getting the group back on subject to get work accomplished. Ling May had been in Miranda's class last year but she hadn't really gotten to know the sweet, dreamy girl until this first cycle. She loved the way Ling May sometimes forget that she was in the classroom instead of a stage and would pirouette across the room.

The yellow group, Josiah, Brent, T.J. and Diana had reached the house first and were already mixing dirt, loose straw, and water into a goopy mixture in a wheel barrow. This adobe mixture was going to be the plaster for the outside of the house.

The goal was to spread the thick mud mixture on in a thin layer, let it dry a bit then spread more layers on top. It made Miranda think of the mud pies she had made with Candy when they were younger.

The chocolate group got their wheel barrow and mixed up their concoction and then it was the red group's turn. Christopher was mixing in the dirt and straw that Miranda and Ling May tossed in while Kelton added water one bucket at a time to make sure it didn't get too watered down. Once the mixture looked right, Christopher wheeled it over to the section of the house they would be working on. At first Miranda had on rubber dishwashing gloves but soon decided they were too hot and awkward. It was easier to just dig in with her hands and give herself a mud bath. She found it oddly relaxing. While they worked, the autumn leaves on the trees surrounding the house were gently raining down on them. Yellow. Red. Orange. It was glorious and Miranda was suddenly overcome with a sense of complete happiness.

The class worked for a few hours then took a break for a picnic lunch. After lunch some of the boys tossed a Frisbee back and forth. Miranda stretched out on the ground, rolled up her jacket and put it under her head. This was normally the time of day that her class had personal reflection time and it seemed like most of the kids wanted to spend some quiet time alone or wanted to crash. Several of them had taken Miranda's lead and found a soft spot to take a nap on.

Miranda thought about Miss Walker's presentation to new middle school parents. She had talked about research showing how similar middle school students were to 3 year olds and daily quiet time or naps were a common need for both ages.

I was sitting on a red and yellow plaid blanket. A small red bird came and sat next to me. The bird started talking, "Water is life. Water is life." Then a cloud overshadowed the blanket and burst into tiny droplets pelting me.

Miranda suddenly realized she was getting wet. Christopher was standing over her flicking water on her. "Wake up sleepy head, its time to get back to work!"

She looked up at the good looking Hispanic boy and said, "O.K., O.K. stop with the water!" as she threw her makeshift pillow at him. She couldn't believe she had fallen into such a deep sleep. She must have been more exhausted than she realized.

The class continued to work through the afternoon. Miranda was surprised by how much they accomplished.

"Many hands make light work." Her mother would have said. Miranda, Charlie, Ling Mae, and Josiah were the last ones to clean up. They had about 30 minutes until the bonfire would really get going. The four students were washing their hands, and putting away the tools their groups had used.

"That was fun work." Ling May said.

"You are right, it was fun. It's amazing that you can build a house of straw bales and mud. It is a pig's dream come true." Josiah said.

The girls laughed. It was good to see Josiah smile.

Charlie and Ling May picked up the water jugs the class had brought with them. They would need to be refilled with ice water for the students to drink the next day. They walked ahead of Josiah and Miranda. Ling May was excitedly talking to Charlie about her upcoming part in the Nutcracker.

Josiah and Miranda walked quietly for a few minutes, but Miranda was glad it wasn't a strained silence. It was more a feeling of calm acceptance.

Miranda almost hated to break the peaceful mood, but she wanted to ask Josiah about Emily while there was no one else listening to their conversation.

"How is Emily doing?" she finally ventured.

"She is still in a coma but the doctors say she is stronger than before. We just have to keep waiting to see what happens. They said she has many broken bones and will have to have a lot of physical therapy when she wakes up, but at least they are saying when instead of if." Josiah let out a long breath as if relieved to have finally said something out loud about the situation.

"I'm sure your family must be very grateful for that." Miranda gently commented.

Josiah looked straight ahead at the path before them as if he were trying to look into the future in some parallel universe.

"It is such a weird thing" he finally whispered.

"Emily and I haven't been what you would really call close. I guess for a long time I resented her. Like it was her fault that my parents got a divorce. My dad left my mom and me and married Emily's mom. Every time I went to their house I wondered why she got to have my dad and the only time I got to see him was on the weekends. I wondered why he loved them more then my mom and me. As I got older though I realized it wasn't really like that and it wasn't Emily's fault. That was our parents' decision. What they did might impact us but it didn't really reflect us. She probably felt angry at us for making her dad go away. Emily is a nice girl, she loves her youth group at her church and she was working at the Bluebird Café to save money to go to Honduras on a mission trip next summer. I feel bad for how I've treated her. I spent all that time being angry with her and then we almost lost her. She may just be my step sister, but she is the only sibling I may ever have, and I really don't want to lose her now."

Miranda didn't know what to say so she just shook her head in agreement. Her father had told her when Charlie first came to the school that sometimes people just need a quiet space before they feel safe enough to talk. Miranda thought about the times when her tiny little blonde friend would sit next to her and they would play side by side without ever saying a thing. She felt like that now, like Josiah just needed someone next to him.

After a couple of minutes Josiah broke the silence. "Thanks Miranda, for listening. This stuff is hard for me to talk about, but you are easy to talk with."

Miranda smiled up at Josiah, it seemed like some of his burden had been lifted. She wondered if he had ever told anyone else about his anger towards Emily and her mom. She felt honored that he trusted her enough to share those feelings with her.

When they reached the campsite they could see that the bonfire had already gotten started. Miranda made her way to where Ling May and Charlie were sitting. The sun had almost set and they were talking about a new movie they both wanted to see. Stephanie walked over to them. "Hey guys, our group finally got the tents all set up so you might want to go put your stuff in before it gets too dark."

"Thanks Steph!" the three girls said in unison as they hopped up to retrieve their sleeping bags and other stuff from the vans. Miranda had been camping a few times with her family but this was really different to be camping with her friends. The girls found the tent marked, "XX" and laughed knowing that the boys' tent was probably marked, "XY", nothing like a little science humor on a class field trip. The girls' tent was a huge three room tent. It had been used on many Peaceful Farm campout trips. The green canvas walls smelled a little bit musty. The temperature had been dropping and the sky was looking a bit cloudy but Miranda guessed the green group had left the windows of the cavernous tent unzipped in hopes of airing it out some. Miranda laid out her pink satin sleeping bag. She put her stuff on top. It looked like the six other girls in the class had already laid claim to the other two rooms so Charlie, Ling May and she took the empty room to the far left.

"Should we zip up the windows?" Charlie asked while looking up at the cloudy sky.

"Perhaps. I don't really want to sleep in a pond tonight." Miranda replied as she tossed her pillow down on her sleeping bag. They zipped up the windows and made their way back to the bonfire.

When they reached the bonfire they saw that the blue group had already laid out the food for the hot dog roast. Miranda grabbed a veggie dog and put it on her stick. She loved roasting food over the campfire. She hoped the blue group had planned on making s'mores for dessert. She liked setting her marshmallow on fire, then blowing it out and smushing it between a square of chocolate and graham crackers. Yum! Why was it that food always tasted better when you were camping?

After they finished with most of the food several people brought out their guitars and they sang for a while. Miranda thought about playing but she was a little bit embarrassed and decided she didn't want to bring that much attention to herself. She looked across the fire and saw that Josiah was talking to Jon. They seemed to be discussing whether or not the fire needed more wood. Josiah looked up and caught Miranda looking at him, she started to turn red, but he flashed a smile at her and she smiled back. She felt warm inside, a good sort of warm. The type of warm that the bonfire could never have given her.

Someone had started singing a song that Miranda recognized as being one of the songs her brother's band sang and she joined in, "Each little step you make is what the journey takes, it is a long, long road and we have far, far to go."

After the bonfire was over they made their way to the tent. Miranda wished they had left the windows down. It was warm and dry inside but it smelled yucky. Sheneca George, one of the other seventh grade girls tried spraying a vanilla scented perfume to help the smell, and that helped a little but the staleness still seemed to linger in the air.

The girls stayed up for a while playing gin rummy by flashlight but they were tired and eventually started dropping off to sleep. Miranda pulled back her pink sleeping bag and snuggled into the soft, gray plaid inside. As she plumped her pillow she could hear Hannah and Carolina giggling about something in the far room. She heard Carolina exclaim, "Oh no he didn't!" then peals of laughter began again.

I picked up the small blue green globe. It seemed to swirl around. It was mesmerizing. I couldn't stop staring at it. It seemed so fragile. Far off I could hear laughter…someone was saying, "You better take care with that. It is very expensive and you won't get another one." I suddenly felt very protective. I needed to find a way to keep it safe. I thought maybe I could wrap it up in something soft but I didn't have anything and I really didn't want to put it away. I wanted to look at it and enjoy it. I just needed to be very careful with it. I started making a cage, some type of structure that would let me enjoy looking at it, but would keep it safe from falling and breaking. I used bamboo and made a small bird cage and put the blue green globe inside. I felt good, like I had done something important and the globe was going to be safe. People started coming into the room. I didn't know who they were, all different types of people, young and old, from all different cultures and they were singing,

"I'd like to build the world a home and furnish it with love.

Grow apple trees and honey bees and snow white turtle doves.

I'd like to teach the world to sing in perfect harmony"

Miranda looked at the globe and then gave it to a small boy wearing a sombrero, he looked at it and then passed it to the beautiful Asian woman next to him, and she passed it to the African warrior next to her. She knew that all of them were responsible then for keeping the fragile globe safe.

The warmth from the sunlight penetrated Miranda's sleepy eyes. She opened them slowly and looked around. The tent was quiet. It seemed like she was the only one awake, and she realized with sudden urgency that she probably needed to find a bathroom pretty fast. She poked her head out of the tent and was glad that the threatening clouds from the night before had passed. Hopefully it would be a beautiful fall day. Miss Walker was outside sitting at the picnic bench by the tent. It looked like she was writing in a journal.

"Good morning Miranda. Did you sleep well?" She softly called out.

"Yes m 'am. I was tired."

"A good day's work usually does give you a good night's sleep." Her teacher smiled at her.

"That is the song from a really famous Coke commercial you are humming by the way. I'm surprised you know it."

Miranda stopped and thought about the tune, "I don't think I consciously knew it, but I dreamed it last night so I guess I've heard it somewhere."

Mrs. Walker winked at her and said, "Reality becomes part of your dreams and your dreams become a part of your reality."

Miranda hurried to the bath house, she was glad she had brought her stuff with her. She hoped being up early would at least give her the advantage of a hot shower.

After she showered and dressed she went back to the picnic table and sat down by her teacher.

"How are you this morning, Miss Walker?"

"I'm doing well. I was just jotting down some reflections of the trip so far so I wouldn't forget them. I also drew a few pictures. Would you like to see them?"

"Definitely" Miranda replied enthusiastically. She remembered that Miss Walker had told them that sometimes when they went on trips they should leave their cameras behind and sketch what they saw because drawing made them look more deeply and think more about their subject then a quick picture allowed for.

Miranda looked at the pen and ink drawings. She saw a picture of two boys she knew would have been Kelton and Christopher hunched over the chess board that had been in the dining hall. There was another one of the green group putting up the tent and then to her surprise one of her and Josiah standing side by side smearing mud on the straw house. She smiled a warm and tingly smile. Miss Walker was a good artist.

"Those are great, thanks for sharing them with me. It makes me want to draw some of my own."

"You should. It is a lot of fun."

That was one of the things Miranda liked about her teacher. She always looked like she was having fun herself so you wanted to join in with her. Suddenly peals of laughter erupted from the tent. Miranda and Miss Walker looked at each other.

"Carolina and Hannah must be awake." Miss Walker said with a grin.

CHAPTER FIVE...Stars

It had been a great week, Miranda thought as the van pulled away from the Hearts and Hands training center. They had ended the week with a reflection time. They had discussed and then written about their service learning at the center. Miss Walker had explained that the difference between doing a service project and doing service learning was that in a project you just went and did something for someone, but service learning was about taking time to reflect on how doing the project had impacted you personally, or the group as a whole. As the group had discussed it, Miranda realized how much closer they had all gotten. Doing the work together had really bonded them. They had done a lot of work on several different projects and the straw house was almost completely finished by the end of the week. It seemed like they all realized that together they had made a difference, and it had been a lot of fun. Miranda had especially enjoyed the hayride they had taken the night before. She had gotten to sit by both Josiah and Charlie and they had been astonished by how brilliant the stars were.

The night sky had seemed so vast and it made her feel so small and insignificant, and yet paradoxically so important as if seeing all those stars made her realize that everything has a place in the universe, even her.

When they had gotten off the wagon Josiah had reached up to help Miranda off. It was a sweet gesture and Miranda was glad she hadn't done another face plant in front of him. His strong hands had been a warm contrast to the cool night air.

Now they were headed home. She was sad to leave, but looking forward to sleeping in her own bed, and seeing Candy. She was surprised to admit to herself how much she had missed her little sister. She had picked up some special rocks from the camp to give to her. It was one of her family's special traditions. Instead of paying for souvenirs from the places they visited they always brought home a rock instead and wrote on them in permanent marker where they were from. She had found some pretty grayish green rocks for the collection. She would have to look them up when they got home to find out what kind they were. Candy would enjoy coming to Hearts and Hands when it was her chance to go on middle school field trips.

CHAPTER SIX...Multi-Cultural Market

Miranda looked at the dry erase board where she had just written all the names of her classmates as they had been drawn out of the special bag Miss Walker kept for the beginning of each cycle when the groups were shuffled around.

Chocolate group: Brent, Diana, Isaac, and Greg

Red group: Hannah, Stephanie, T.J., and Amy

Yellow group: Malcolm, Josiah, Toby, and Kelton

Green group: Christopher, Charlie, Ling May, and Miranda

Blue group: Sheneca, Caroline, Jon, and Steven

That was funny, with the exception of Charlie taking the place of Kelton, she was basically in the same group she had been in during the first cycle. Miss Walker said that since the groups were always drawn randomly that if you got some of the same people in your group twice that it was the universe's way of telling you that you still had something to learn from those people. She was happy that Charlie was in her group this time, and she also had to admit that even though she would have liked to have had Josiah as the eighth grade leader of her group, Christopher was pretty nice and he was certainly nice to look at. She grinned at that thought. She wondered what he thought about being the only boy in the group. She figured Charlie would be happy, she suspected Charlie had a tiny bit of a crush on the eighth grade boy. Once she had told Miranda that he reminded her of Johnny

Depp. Charlie had a thing for old Johnny Depp movies. She wanted to be a pirate when she grew up or at least an actress that played a female pirate opposite of Johnny Depp.

This cycle was "Structures" and they were going to be studying the political structures in the world. Each group would choose a country to study and on Halloween they would have a big multi-cultural market with the rest of the classes of the school and dress up in traditional costumes of the country they had studied. The green group decided to study Ireland. It had a unique political structure. Miranda knew that most of the island was considered "The Republic of Ireland" but the smaller Northern part was still considered a part of Great Britain. She looked forward to learning more about it. She was already thinking ahead to what kind of costumes they could wear and she was pretty sure she could snag some Celtic music for them to play at their booth from Matthew's CD collection.

One of the things she really liked about the way the middle school was set up was that they spent two weeks studying a social world topic in depth and then the next two weeks they studied a science topic in depth. They had other subjects like math and language everyday but it was fun really having time to put a lot of energy into social world activities. She loved studying something and getting to know it really well and this was going to be fun to research. The main topic they were researching was the political structure but learning the history and culture of the country was suppose to help them figure out why that country had organized into a particular political structure.

First the group brainstormed about everything they already knew about Ireland, and then they wrote down all the things they wanted to learn. They decided they wanted to know about the physical features of the island, the religious background, the political history, the foods and clothing, and cultural aspects such as music and art.

Ling May wanted to study the cultural aspects, she already knew about something they did called, "Riverdance". She had seen a traveling group that did that type of dancing that had come to the FedEx Forum in Memphis. Her parents had taken her to see them perform.

Charlie said she would research the religious background and the physical features of the island. Christopher said he would do the political history and so that left food and clothing for Miranda. Miranda seemed to remember something about a potato famine in Ireland so she thought she should start there. They headed to the computers and started their research. Miranda found several great sites and it made her want to go to Ireland for real. It looked so beautiful and green. She understood why it was called "The Emerald Isle." She stopped her research for a moment to pause and look around the room. Everyone was busy doing research. A few people were talking about the things they were learning. It was one of those moments that she really enjoyed being in school, everyone was working together and everyone was learning. It was fun. Most people didn't think of school as fun, but Miranda realized that it really could be fun.

The day sped by and before she knew it Miranda was in her kitchen putting away the dishes after supper before going up to work on her homework. The phone rang. Miranda reached over the white counter top and picked up the cordless black phone.

"Hello, Cockrum residence." Miranda politely answered the phone. It was the way her parents had taught her to answer it when she was little and it had been a hard habit to break even if it did sound a little old fashioned to her.

"Hey, Miranda, it's me, Josiah."

Miranda was a little surprised to hear his voice, and tried to sound calm.

"Hey Josiah, what's up?" She hoped cool and calm was how she sounded, and not flustered and unsure like she felt.

"We just got the news that Emily woke up from her coma. I was so happy I just wanted to tell someone."

"That is wonderful Josiah. I am so glad. Have you seen her yet?"

"No, they just called to let us know. I had made a CD for her of her favorite songs and she just woke up and said, "Turn it up please." It made me feel great, like maybe I did something that helped her wake up."

"That is really cool. Thanks for calling and letting me know. Are you going to see her tonight?"

"Yep, as soon as my mom gets home she is going to take me. I was home alone working on the multi-cultural project when they called me."

"Ah, what country is your group studying?"

"We are studying the Bahamas."

"That sounds like fun. We are doing Ireland. I hope your visit with Emily goes well."

"It will be really good just to see her awake…Miranda, thanks for being my friend."

Miranda didn't know what to say. What she wanted to say was, "You are welcome and feel free to call me every day for the rest of your life." But what she actually said was, "You are welcome Josiah, I consider it an honor to be your friend. Tell Emily hello for me."

"I will, and I will talk to you tomorrow. Bye."

"Bye, Josiah."

Miranda hung up the phone. She was really glad that Emily had woken up, she knew how much that meant to Josiah, and she was thrilled that Josiah had called her. She had never gotten a call from a boy before, even if it was just a friendship call. She clapped her hands did a little twirl and quickly put up the dishes.

Later Miranda was staring at the computer screen looking up Irish recipes when her dad came in.

"Oh, good I see you are planning to start cooking the meals around here."

Miranda laughed, "Not quite yet dad. I am doing research for our country for the multi-cultural market. We are studying Ireland and I'm in charge of looking up food."

"Ireland. How appropriate!" Peter Cockrum said while tugging on his red hair.

"Of course. Aren't we actually from Ireland?"

"I think so. In fact it is sort of an interesting story. The first immigrant to America from our family was actually a woman and her last name was Cockrum."

"Wait a minute, was she a widow? Were her children with her?"

"Nope."

"Apparently she was a beautiful girl and when she came to this country a lad with the last name of Dunlap wanted to marry her, but she wouldn't give up her family's coat of arms to marry him so he changed his name to Cockrum and they settled down and had a family." Peter grinned.

"Wow that is a great story."

"Yep, I have done a little bit of research and the Cockrum family seems to come from England, but the red hair our family passes down and the story makes me think that she must have been a transplant to England from Ireland somehow, perhaps her family had immigrated there during the potato famine."

"The potato famine, I have been doing a little bit of research on that. I found a song by a singer named Sinead O'Connor that seemed pretty incriminating towards the English about the potato famine. She claimed that there really wasn't a famine, but the English took most of the rest of the food from the Irish people and left them with only potatoes to eat and the potatoes had been hit by some type of disease that made them rot. The potato famine was apparently the reason a lot of Irish people immigrated to other countries, especially America."

Peter stroked his beard, "It is interesting how things happen isn't it? A bad thing can sometimes lead to a good thing; the pages of history turn quickly."

"I guess so, and I better get back to my research so I can get my project done quickly."

"Yep. Hey, Matthew called a little while ago and he is planning on coming home for Halloween."

"Goodie! Is anyone coming with him?" Miranda was hoping he would bring home Daniel, one of the other band members. Daniel was a lot of fun, always cracking jokes and making her laugh.

"I don't know. I forgot to ask and he didn't mention anyone."

Miranda turned back to her research after her dad left the room. She liked the story of the pretty Irish girl who a man was willing to give up his family name for. She would have to remember to tell Matthew that story. He would probably turn it into a song.

At 9:00 Miranda cut off the computer and headed upstairs. She grabbed her guitar and sat on her bed. She loved playing her guitar. It relaxed her and made her happy. She spent a while working on a song she had hoped to perfect before Matthew came home. She was getting better but she knew she would have to practice some more. She put the guitar on the stand her dad had made for her and turned out the light, snuggled into her bed and fell fast asleep.

I looked down the tube of a pirate's scope. Everywhere around there was water. The boat rocked gently. To the left of me was a bunch of wooden crates labeled, "Rum" and a picture of a rooster on them. I was eating French fries. Someone was walking toward me. It was Matthew. He had his guitar. He was singing something about a girl named Maggie. He looked really happy. I shared my French fries with him. Candy walked toward us. She was being followed by a little white dog. Matthew started to whistle and the dog started barking at him. Matthew just laughed at him.

What was that noise? Ugh. The neighbor's dog. Its name was Tiger but they all just referred to it as "Yappy". Why were little dogs so annoying when they barked? Miranda rolled over and looked at the neon green numbers of the clock, "11:11" She turned over and went back to sleep. When morning came she woke up and got dressed quicker than usual. She was looking forward to the multi-cultural market.

Miranda turned up the CD a little louder; she was sitting on a stool next to the booth that the green group had created for Ireland. The samples of baked potatoes she had made to give out were a success. Charlie had made a replica of the physical island of Ireland out of clay. A small castle perched on top. There were several big fold out posters. Ling May had gotten pictures of the Riverdance group and some art work by artists from Ireland. Christopher had done a poster of the political structure. Miranda felt like they had worked well together and she learned a lot about the country.

She looked around the yard. Across from her booth was the yellow group's booth about the Bahamas. She looked at Josiah and waved. He had told her that Emily was improving every day. Their booth had a big fake palm tree beside it with a plastic pink flamingo underneath it. It looked like they were serving some type of rice dish. Malcolm had a big straw hat on his head. Toby and Kelton were sitting behind some type of big drum beating on it.

The school had invited parents and other visitors to the market. It was also a fund raiser for the school with each booth making some type of small item from their country to sell. Miranda's group had made little crocheted lace ornaments that were shaped like shamrocks. Candy's class had done Russia and had made small paper mache stacking dolls. They were really cute. Miranda hoped to make it over to the Belgium booth, they were serving chocolate for their food. She laughed as Ling May started dancing an Irish jig for a crowd of people that had gathered.

In the crowd she saw a tall, voluptuous girl with short dark hair that she didn't recognize. She seemed to be college age. After Ling May finished her jig, the tall girl walked towards Miranda. The girl was wearing earrings in the shape of guitars. She smiled at Miranda, and Miranda smiled back, the girl stuck out her hand and said, "Hello, I'm Meghan. Are you Miranda Cockrum?"

Miranda hesitantly answered yes. The smiling girl said, "I thought I recognized you from Matthew's description."

Miranda was confused. "Do you know Matthew?"

"Yep. We go to college together. I sing for his band sometimes."

"Is Matthew here?" Miranda squealed.

Just then Miranda's green eyed brother appeared behind Meghan.

"Matthew!" Miranda exclaimed and gave her big brother a big hug. It seemed like forever since she had seen him.

"Hey sis! I see you already met Meghan." Matthew looked at the pretty college girl standing next to him and in that instant Miranda knew that Meghan was not just a casual friend to Matthew.

"Yes, she said she recognized me from your description. I hope you said nice things about me."

"I just told her the truth, and you know how honest I am." He said in a teasing voice. "I hope you don't mind, but I also told her how kind and generous you are, and how willing to share your room with her you would be." Matthew grinned.

"Sure Matthew." Miranda grinned back at him and socked him in the arm. She whirled around and gave Meghan an impromptu hug.

"I would be delighted to have you bunk with me Meghan as long as you don't mind clutter and a carpet of dirty clothes."

"No problem. I'm just glad to have a place to lay my head." Meghan responded.

Matthew gave Miranda another hug and told her he would see her later. They were going to check out the rest of the booths and see which one had the best food.

Miranda watched in amazement as Matthew and Meghan joined hands and walked away. Matthew had never had a serious girlfriend before even though there had been lots of girls who had liked him. Meghan must have been very special to have caught his eye. She looked forward to getting to know her.

That night after supper they all sat around the table and talked for a long time. Meghan seemed to fit into their family as if she had always been there. She was a music major and had met Matthew one night when he came to her senior recital with a friend of hers. Matthew said he was blown away with what a beautiful voice she had and the easy way she related to the audience and so he had asked her to sing with his band a few times. Only a few times though he joked because she didn't really fit in with the band name and "Green Eyed Boys and A Hazel Eyed Girl" was too long of a name.

Meghan laughed at him. Later that night Meghan asked Miranda if it would be o.k. if she played her guitar. Miranda nodded her head yes and Meghan picked it up and started tuning it. Then

Meghan began to play. It was a slow song and
Matthew was right, Meghan had an amazing voice.
It was strong but sweet. She sang a song by Nora
Jones. She also played the guitar really well. After
that song she sang an Allison Krauss song.

In between the private concert Meghan told
Miranda a little bit about her life. She had grown
up in Texas and her father had been a music teacher
at a small college. She could have gone to school
there but she decided she wanted to try to go to a
bigger school and had been offered a full ride to Old
Miss. She would be graduating in May and hoped
to get a job singing in musicals, or maybe find a
good band that needed a lead vocalist. Miranda
knew Matthew still had another year in school. She
wondered how he felt about Meghan being older
and graduating before him.

Miranda knew Matthew had always talked
about going to New York and trying to break into
the art scene there, maybe Meghan would go ahead
of him and find something to do on Broadway.
Miranda tried to imagine their life together…but
maybe she was letting her imagination run too wild.

"So do you like Matthew a lot?" she asked
tentatively, not even sure what she hoped the
answer would be.

Meghan smiled at her. "I do like him a lot.
I haven't dated very much; mostly I have watched
guys and thought, no thanks-better to be alone than
wish I was alone! Matthew was different to me
though. There was something so unique and the
first time we went out, we talked for hours without
ever stopping."

Miranda thought about her brother. She had
always admired him but sometimes his mood

swings had been obnoxious. She wondered if he was ever like that around Meghan.

Meghan taught Miranda how to play a simple song on the guitar, "I'm Leaving on a Jet Plane". Miranda practiced it for a while when Meghan went down to use the shower before bedtime. It had been a good day, but Miranda was very sleepy. She hoped she didn't snore with Meghan in the room.

The table I was standing next to was covered with a white lace cloth. It had a big brown stain on it. I felt compelled to try and scrub the stain clean, but no matter how hard I scrubbed it didn't seem to get clean, it just seemed to get darker and bigger. I wondered if there was any way to clean it off. Then my classmates started coming in the room. We all sat down at the table. Servants started walking in carrying plates of food. The food was placed on the table and it covered up the stain. Toby stood up and said a blessing for the food. It was a sweet prayer, a prayer about unity and the need for each of us to walk gently on the earth. I said, "Amen" and then started putting the food on my plate, but instead of feeding myself I reached over and started feeding the girl next to me. Music was playing in the background it was an Elvis song...I listened closer...Matthew's band had played this song once before, "Jail House Rock". There was a loud noise it sounded like a shot and then everyone was screaming and jumping up and running away.

Miranda sat straight up in bed. Tinkerbelle said 12:00. She hadn't been asleep very long. She could hear the television on downstairs. She felt thirsty so she crept down the stairs to get a drink. She saw Meghan and her mom and Matthew watching a movie in the living room. It looked like an old murder mystery and Miranda debated about watching it with them but decided to go back to bed. As she reached her room she glanced over at the book she was supposed to be reading for school, *1984*. It was actually an interesting book; she just hadn't had very much time to read it. Maybe she could read it some tomorrow. She loved Saturdays!

CHAPTER SEVEN…Walking In One Another's Shoes

Miranda sat in community meeting on Monday morning. It was her turn to be the observer. She didn't really like being the observer she felt like "Big Brother". She hated telling on people at the end of the meeting. She knew it wasn't really meant to come across that way, but it still felt the same. Luckily everyone was pretty calm that morning, except for Hannah and Carolina who had been talking while T.J. was sharing a story about going to the mall that weekend and seeing someone he thought was Kobe Bryant but turned out to just be a really tall man. She thought she heard Hannah say something about the pants she had bought at the mall that weekend for $9.99. She seemed pretty proud of her purchase.

After the meeting was over, Miss Walker told them about an activity they would be doing outside of school hours called, "Walking in One Another's Shoes." It was a part of the Heroic Journey program they were doing as a personal world program that year. The activity didn't mean they were literally going to be walking in somebody else's shoes; it meant that they would be spending the day at someone else's house who they didn't normally hang out with.

Miranda looked around the room at her classmates. Most of them were pretty familiar to her since they had all gone to school together for so long. Miranda wondered who Miss Walker would pair her up with. She listened intently as Miss Walker called out the names. Charlie was paired up with the new girl Amy. Josiah was paired up with Jon. Miranda was paired up with Sheneca.

Miranda sort of cringed. There was nothing wrong with Sheneca. Miranda didn't mind being paired up with her, it was her little brother who Miranda didn't want to deal with. Jeffrey Jones was a pain. Just that morning he had let Midnight out from her cage and Miranda had been the one who had to chase the bunny down to get her back in the cage. Miranda was pretty sure he had done it on purpose. He also had a way of saying her name in a sing song voice that made her want to throttle him. Miranda wondered how Sheneca managed to deal with such an obnoxious kid brother.

Miss Walker told them to spend a few minutes talking with each other. It seemed like the Friday night after next would be the best time for them to get together at Sheneca's house. Sheneca would come to her house the following Saturday night. Miranda made a mental note to clean her room. She wondered what type of things Sheneca liked to do. Miss Walker said that they weren't supposed to do anything out of the ordinary. Anything that the host normally did like chores or whatever, the guest needed to do them also to get an idea of what it was like to be in the other person's life. It made Miranda think of it as an anthropology experiment. Sheneca would probably be glad that she wasn't coming over on a trash pick-up day. She wondered if Sheneca had any obnoxious chores…she hoped babysitting wasn't one of them.

CHAPTER EIGHT...Sheneca

Miranda looked around her room. She spent several hours cleaning and rearranging. According to Tinkerbelle, Sheneca should arrive any minute. Miranda wondered how Sheneca would feel about an afternoon nap, she was exhausted. Cleaning was way more work than it was worth. She looked out the window to see a blue van pull up. She walked down stairs and made it to the door just as the bell rang. Sheneca and her dad stood on the front porch. Her dad was carrying a pink and black checkered overnight bag for Sheneca.

Katura rounded the corner of the living room. "Hello Mr. Jones! Thanks for bringing Sheneca over. I think they are going to have a good time."

The short, stocky man on the porch nodded and said, "Yep, I imagine they will. Just have her give me a call in the morning and I will swing by and pick her up."

He handed the checkered bag to Sheneca and reminded her to, "Behave." Then he waved good bye and headed back to the blue van.

Miranda showed Sheneca around the downstairs of the house then they poked their heads into Candy's room.

"Sheneca!" Candy exclaimed. The red headed girl jumped up from the doll house she was playing with. She was wearing a blue polka dotted dress with a pair of purple tights. "Would you like to see my doll house? My daddy made it for me."

Sheneca walked over to the big Victorian style house. It was really beautiful and Miranda knew that even adult females were tempted to play with it. Sheneca and Candy sat down for a few minutes so Candy could show her all the special details of the house.

Sheneca listened patiently and told Candy how much she liked the house. They moved the furniture around a little bit and Candy told her all about the inhabitants of the house. A family very similar to their own with three kids, a mom and dad, only in Candy's imaginary house there were all sorts of little animals also…even a small brown pony tied up in the back yard. Miranda wasn't sure if Sheneca was really enjoying herself or just being really polite. She told Candy that they would come back later but they needed to go put Sheneca's stuff away.

Miranda and Sheneca made their way up to Miranda's room. Sheneca smiled really big when she saw the room.

"What an awesome room Miranda. I love the sky light. That is so cool." They stored Sheneca's stuff in the closet and decided to get out a monopoly game to play for a while. Candy knocked softly on the door.

"Can I play too?" she asked timidly.

Sheneca said, "Sure." Then she looked up at Miranda as if to make sure she hadn't spoken too fast.

"That's fine, Candy, do you want to be the dog or the wheel barrow?" Miranda laughed already knowing the answer. Candy always chose the dog.

They played until supper time and then went down for a meal of bean soup and homemade bread. It smelled so good. Miranda hadn't realized how hungry she was.

After supper they did the dishes and then went into the living room to see if there was anything they wanted to watch. There wasn't anything good on so Miranda asked Sheneca if she had ever seen the movie, *Princess Bride*. She hadn't so they decided to watch it. It was Miranda's favorite movie and she could watch it over and over again. Sheneca liked the movie and for the rest of the night as they talked they would make references back to the movie. As they were walking up the stairs Sheneca stopped at the picture of Katura and Peter on their wedding day and said, "Wuv, Tru Wuv…" and made Miranda burst into giggles. They went upstairs and gossiped about different things going on at school and Sheneca told her how lucky she was to have such a sweet little sister.

"My little brother can be a real brat." Sheneca confided. Miranda already knew this but didn't want to be rude and agree too much. She knew it was one thing to complain about a family member but quite another to have someone else complain about your family member.

Still hearing Sheneca talk about her brother made her worry even more about what it would be like to walk in Sheneca's shoes and spend the night in the same house as the brat.

Miranda cautiously said, "Why do you think he is like that?"

"Well, when he was little my mom got really sick for a long time and I don't think she really had the energy to make him behave. After she died I think my dad was grieving too much to really pay attention to him the way he needed."

Miranda was amazed that Sheneca had said that in such a matter of fact way. Miranda had no idea her mother had died. Come to think of it, at any of the functions at school it had only been

Sheneca's dad there, but Miranda had never really given it much thought before.

"Sheneca, I'm so sorry, I didn't know that your mother wasn't alive."

"Umm, it is o.k. it happened a long time ago. I have a few memories of her but not very many so I guess I don't really know any difference."

Miranda was quiet. She thought about her own mother and how much of her life revolved around her, about how much she meant to their family. She really couldn't imagine life without her mom. She felt really sad for Sheneca. She wondered what she had died from but didn't know if she should ask. Finally Sheneca broke the awkward silence by saying, "I like your guitar. Can you play something for me?"

Miranda was glad to have a chance to redeem herself. She picked up the guitar and played the new song that Meghan had just taught her. Sheneca really liked it. Miranda asked her if she knew how to play and Sheneca said no but she had always wondered how. Miranda taught her a few of the basics and they spent the rest of the night playing with the guitar and talking about school. Miranda confessed her crush on Josiah and Sheneca told Miranda that she sort of had a crush on Toby. Toby was nice, she thought Sheneca and he would look good together.

"Wuv, Tru Wuv." They both said at the same time and burst into another round of giggles.

In the morning the smell of pancakes and sausage drifted up to the room waking up the girls and tempting them out of bed.

"I thought your parents didn't eat meat. I hope they didn't buy sausage just for me." Sheneca announced.

Miranda laughed, "We like you Sheneca but not enough to buy meat for you. It is actually veggie sausage. It is made with soy and stuff. Try it and tell me what you think. I've never had meat so I don't know how it compares to the real thing."

The girls dressed quickly and hurried down the stairs. Miranda heard Pachelbel's Cannon on the CD player in the kitchen. It was one of her mom's favorite pieces. Her mom had told her once that they had played it at their wedding reception. Sheneca's eyes got really big when she saw the food piled on the table.

"Wow. This beats pop tarts."

Sheneca thought the veggie sausage tasted pretty good, but she loved the pancakes covered with blueberry syrup. She looked like she was in heaven. Candy came in the room still in her pajamas. She had on a large white shirt with a big smiley face she had painted herself and a pair of pajama pants that had a small print of teddy bears all over them. Candy looked sleepy but she smiled a big smile when she saw that Sheneca was still there.

She started telling Sheneca some jokes and riddles, "Sheneca, what do you get when you cross a bridge with a bicycle?"

Miranda knew the answer because it was one of Candy's favorite jokes, but Sheneca looked puzzled.

"I'm not sure-maybe a bricycle?"

"Nope, you just get to the other side!" Candy let out a silly giggle with the answer to the riddle.

"That is pretty funny." Sheneca held up her hand and gave a small little wave, "Do you know what this is?"

Candy grinned at her and said, "Nope."

Sheneca grinned back and said, "It is a micro-wave!"

Candy nearly fell off the chair laughing. They spent the rest of breakfast trading jokes back and forth. After breakfast Sheneca called her dad to pick her up. As her dad's blue van pulled up she thanked Miranda for letting her come over.

"I had a really great time. I'm looking forward to having you come over to my house next week…just be prepared for cold cereal though…I'm not as good a cook as your mom!"

Miranda puzzled over that last statement after Sheneca left. She wondered if Sheneca did most of the cooking since her mom had died. Miranda went to the kitchen where her mom was still cleaning up.

"Did you have fun with Sheneca?" her mom asked.

"Yeah, it was a lot of fun. I'm glad we did it because I knew her, but not that well. Now I feel like she is a good friend. She is really nice." Miranda said as she sniffed the vanilla spray perfume that Sheneca had shared with her that morning. Miranda looked at her mom and then impulsively jumped up and gave her a hug.

"I love you mom." She said.

"I love you too, Miranda, and I'm glad that y'all had a good time together. I imagine Sheneca's life must be slightly different from yours since Miss Walker put the two of you together. I imagine you will learn even more about her since you will be staying at her house next week."

"Yes. I guess so. I may take some rope and tie up her little brother though." Miranda teased.

Katura laughed, "Jeffrey can be a handful, but I'm sure you can handle him even if I make you leave the rope behind."

"Aw, mom!" Miranda laughed.

CHAPTER NINE...The Sun and the Wind

Miss Walker passed out the study guides that the class would be using for Personal World reflection activities. Isaac flipped his bright orange hair out of his eyes and started reading the overview aloud. Miranda stared at the freckles dotting Isaac's face as he read the story of the sun and the wind having a competition to get some guy to take off his coat. The wind blew really hard which made the guy pull his coat closer and the sun gently warmed him up so he took the coat off. Miss Walker asked them what they thought the coat represented. Toby observed that it might be the guards that we put up against the world and that the sun didn't try to pressure the guy he just gently lead him to let go of his defenses.

Miranda looked up at Sheneca and they smiled at each other. Miranda felt privileged that Sheneca told her about the crush she had on Toby. Toby was a really nice guy; she thought Sheneca had good taste.

As a class they discussed the rest of the study guide and Miss Walker explained that soon each of them would need to find a mentor, someone older than them that they could talk to and get advice from for the rest of the school year. She suggested they look for a mentor who would lead them like the sun, gently guiding them and helping them to make good decisions for the future. She also told them to achieve balance in life it was always good to not only have a mentor, but also to be a mentor and that the other teachers would be giving her a list soon of younger students that they felt might need extra encouragement for one reason or another and the middle school students would be choosing someone from that list to mentor.

Miranda started thinking about who she would like to have as a mentor. No one came to mind immediately but maybe as she worked through some of the questions on her study guide it would help her figure it out. She liked reflection time. Her writing here was less structured than essays and she could put down her thoughts without worrying about grammar or spelling. It gave her a chance to think about big things in her life in a methodical way. She liked reading back through her reflection journal: seeing the doodles, random notes, and poems she had written. It helped her to see her thoughts in black and white…and purple, pink, green, and yellow…she liked the way using colored pencils and markers jazzed up the thoughts in her journal. She enjoyed imagining that her thoughts had beautiful lives of their own.

After school that day Miranda and Charlie sat on the white swing on Charlie's porch and talked about who they might choose as mentors. Charlie had decided that she would like to ask Amber Jones, a college student who worked at the hospital with her mom. Talking about the hospital made Miranda think about the last time she had been there and her encounter with Josiah. She was glad that Emily seemed to be doing better. Every once in a while when no one was around Miranda would ask Josiah about Emily. He said she was going through physical therapy now and even though it was really hard on her it seemed to be making a big difference. She wasn't at home yet but had been moved to a rehabilitation center so when he went to his dad's house they would go there to see her. Josiah said he made her some more mixed CDs and she seemed to really like them. Miranda wondered if Emily would like the new recording the Green Eyed Boys had just put out. Matthew was excited about it and the sound quality was good even if the band had just used Matt's computer to put it together. Miranda had noticed that Meghan's voice could be heard in some of the backgrounds of the songs.

Miranda's mom picked her up at five and they drove to pick up Candy from her art lesson at Mrs. Love's house. Miranda was looking forward to seeing little Zoe. As they entered the knotty pine hallway of the Love's house they saw that Zoe was asleep in a small wooden cradle. She looked adorable in a pink ruffled sleeper. Candy was cleaning up her paint brushes and quickly put away the painting she was working on. Miranda had the feeling that Candy might be painting something special as a Christmas gift for their parents.

Miranda missed her former teacher but was glad that Candy's private lessons allowed her to see her on a weekly basis. Mrs. Love gave her a hug and told her there were peanut butter balls on the counter if she wanted some. Mrs. Love used to bring the peanut butter balls to class when she taught at Peaceful Farm and she knew Miranda had a fondness for them. Reaching for the delicious snack Miranda suddenly realized exactly who she wanted as a mentor. She quietly got her mom's attention to ask if it would be o.k. and her mom smiled to let her know she approved the choice. Miranda realized it was a big deal to ask someone to be a mentor for you, and Mrs. Love might be too busy with taking care of Zoe but she hoped she would say yes.

CHAPTER TEN...Peanut Butter Balls

Watching out for the yellow mums on the side of the driveway Miranda made her way to the Prius being careful to not spill the platter of peanut butter balls she had made from Mrs. Love's recipe. Mrs. Love had told her that she would be honored to be her mentor and she had even given her the peanut butter ball recipe so Miranda could make some to take to Sheneca's house. They were easy to make: 1/3 cup peanut butter, 1/3 cup of honey, and 2/3 cup of powdered milk, just mix it all together and form into balls. An easy enough recipe that hopefully even Miranda couldn't mess it up. She hoped Sheneca would like them.

Sheneca's house was on Oak Street, two streets down from Charlie's house. Miranda wondered if Charlie realized how close she lived to Sheneca. The house was a brick ranch style house typical of a lot of the houses in this area of town. The house had three small bedrooms and a back yard with a trampoline. Miranda and Sheneca decided to go jump on the trampoline for a while. They made up silly games to play like trying to sing "Twinkle, Twinkle, Little Star" as they jumped in the air to see how far they got before they landed. It was fun. Miranda had never jumped on a trampoline very much. After a while they stopped jumping and just sat cross legged on the trampoline and gossiped. Mostly they talked about Stephanie Westwood and her tendency to flirt with all the boys in class, especially Christopher and Josiah. Sheneca reassured Miranda that while she had noticed that Josiah was nice to Stephanie, he didn't seem too flattered by her attention. Sheneca had a Facebook account like several of the middle school students and she had noticed that Josiah and Stephanie were friends and Stephanie had written on his wall a lot but Josiah didn't respond that much. Miranda wished her parents would let her get a Facebook account but they felt like she was too young and they wanted her to have real conversations with her peers not just virtual ones.

After a while they decided they were hungry and wanted a snack so they went inside to indulge in the peanut butter balls. When they entered the cheerful red and yellow kitchen though, they discovered the platter with the peanut butter balls was missing. At the same time they both exclaimed, "Jeffrey!" Sure enough they found him in front of the TV in the living room playing video games with the empty platter in front of them. He looked up at them and said, "Thanks for the peanut butter balls. They were delicious!"

Miranda was pretty sure Sheneca could have throttled her brother but she just took a deep breath, looked at Miranda, and whispered an apologetic, "I'm sorry!" Miranda wasn't sure how to respond so she just shrugged her shoulders, "That is o.k. they are really easy to make, now that you know he likes them I'll show you how so you can make more for him."

"Speaking of making things I better get dinner together, dad will be home soon." Sheneca sighed.

Miranda followed her into the kitchen and watched as Sheneca pulled out a big pot, filled it with water and set it on the stove to boil.

"I hope you like pasta because that is the only vegetarian thing I could think of to make."

"I love pasta. I love the way it can be so different depending on what you put with it."

"Definitely, I was thinking of an Alfredo sauce which is a white sauce, but I also have a red marinara sauce, or I can make up a pesto sauce with olive oil, basil and pine nuts. Which would you prefer Madame?" Sheneca giggled.

"Wow, what an assortment of choices. I feel like I am at a four star restaurant." Miranda teased. She could tell Sheneca felt really comfortable in the kitchen and probably enjoyed impressing her. "I'll take the white sauce please, and do you have anything to drink while I watch the master chef at work?"

"Certainly my dear, we have the sweetest of sweet tea or the grapiest of grape Kool Aid. Your wish is my command."

"Sweet tea please, with a touch of ice if that is possible."

Miranda sat at the tall counter and watched as Sheneca put together their meal. She could tell that Sheneca knew exactly what she was doing; she didn't even use a sauce out of the jar. She mixed together some type of cream and butter and different kinds of cheeses. Watching Sheneca in the kitchen amazed her since putting together peanut butter balls had been a big deal to Miranda.

"How did you learn to cook Sheneca?" Miranda said as she swirled the ice in her sweet tea.

"T.V. mostly, I watch a lot of cooking shows, and I have a few of my mom's old cook books. It was a matter of desperation actually. My dad is a horrible cook and I decided if I wanted to eat more than fried eggs and hot dogs I would have to teach myself. I'm not as good a cook as your mom and I do still eat a lot of pop tarts and cold cereal but I like making big meals at night for my dad."

Miranda paused not sure if she should ask her next question or not, "Does your dad miss your mom a lot?"

Sheneca plopped some garlic bread in the oven before she answered. "Yes, we all do, he has never even dated anyone else. I know he is lonely but I guess work and keeping up with the house and us…especially Jeffrey…is about all he has the energy for."

Miranda paused then said, "How would you feel about it if he did find someone else to date or marry?"

Sheneca smiled, "I don't know, it has been just us for so long, it might be a little weird to have someone else around, although when I was at your house I admit it was really nice to be the one not cooking for once! So I hope if he does meet someone else not only will she will love my dad, but also be a good cook, and be able to handle Jeffrey."

Miranda thought about that kind of woman and wondered where she could be found. She also wondered if it was a natural instinct for all girls to be match makers.

CHAPTER 11...Jeffrey

After she spent the night at Sheneca's house Miranda had noticed a change in her attitude toward Jeffrey. She even surprised herself by choosing Jeffrey to be the elementary child she would be willing to mentor. She started to understand that a lot of the times he was choosing to be a brat it was out of habit and in an effort to get attention. She wondered if she gave him positive attention if he might be a little calmer.

Miss Walker gave them time on Friday afternoons to go spend some time with the students they were mentoring. Miranda helped Jeffrey with the spelling words he had missed on his test from the morning. As they were working on them she noticed that he often just mixed up the letters in the words. Falcon had been written faclon, and mountain had become moutnain. It made her wonder if Jeffrey might be dyslexic, she would have to remember to ask his teacher about that privately.

Miranda saw that the words had been taken from the novel the students had been reading in class, *My Side of the Mountain* by Jean Craighead George. She remembered her mom reading that story to her when she was younger. Her mom had told her that when Matthew read it he had decided to live in his tree house for a few weeks, but he snuck in frequently for snacks and TV breaks. Miranda asked Jeffrey what he thought of the book. He said he liked it and thought it would be cool to live in a tree and have a pet falcon but he wouldn't want to be away from his family. Miranda smiled at him. She was glad she had decided to spend more time with Jeffrey, maybe he really did have a good side. She was even more impressed when he told her thanks when they had finished working on the spelling corrections, then of course he grinned and asked her when she was going to make him some more peanut butter balls.

When the school day ended Miranda walked back to her locker and got the new book they were reading for this cycle. It was a collection of the speeches and letters of Martin Luther King Jr. Miranda was looking forward to reading it.

They were going to be taking a field trip to the Civil Rights Museum in Memphis during their immersion week this cycle and she wanted to read more about this dynamic man who had been shot at the hotel in Memphis that had been turned into the museum. She was curious about what drove him to speak up for other people and his belief that people could change their hearts. When she had been at Sheneca's house she had seen pictures of Sheneca's grandparents walking in marches. Sheneca's grandfather had been one of the garbage workers that had been in Memphis at the time of Martin Luther King Jr.'s murder. Seeing those pictures on the wall of her friend's house had made history seem a lot less distant.

She was also excited because she was going to get to see Susan tonight. It had been a busy year and it had been hard for them to get together. Susan was a cheerleader at East Middle and she seemed to always been heading out for practice or at a game when Miranda had called but finally they were going to be able to get together. Susan's church had something they called fifth quarter so they were going to the Pete's Grove high school football game and then going to the church afterwards to play games and eat snacks. Miranda wondered about what it would be like in two years when they would be able to go to the same high school. It would be very different to have all her peers from Peaceful Farm and her friends from soccer and scouts and other places at the same place. It would be a uniting of the different spheres of her life. She wondered if Susan and Charlie would be friends. They had never really done anything together. Charlie was shy and meeting new people was hard for her sometimes. They had met at Miranda's birthday parties but they didn't seem to have a lot in common. Susan was very into sports, being socially aware, and being the center of attention. Charlie, well, Charlie was just Charlie.

CHAPTER 12...Being in the Game

Everyone was in a good mood. Pete's Grove high school had won their final football game. As Susan and Miranda walked down the corridor of the church building leading to the gym Miranda noticed a bulletin board on the wall that said, "Pray for Emily" underneath were two pictures of a pretty blonde girl. In one of the pictures the girl was in hiking gear and was flashing a peace sign, in the other she was in a hospital bed. Emily. Emily Hunter, Josiah's sister. She must go to Susan's church. Miranda stopped in front of the board and asked Susan if she knew her.

"Yes, she is really smart and sweet. It was so sad about the accident. We have been praying for her and doing some fund raisers to help her parents with the hospital bills. Do you know her?"

"Her step-brother, Josiah, goes to my school."

"Of course! Josiah. Your Josiah." Then Susan grinned at her and winked.

Miranda hadn't thought about the hospital bills that must be piling up. All the therapy Emily was going through must be expensive. She wondered if there was anything she could do to help Emily's family.

The girls walked into the gym. Several boys were playing basketball and there was a long table in the corner with snacks and drinks. Susan started chatting with a middle aged woman standing next to the table. Susan introduced Miranda to the woman. Her name was Terri and she started asking Miranda all the usual questions grown-ups ask about school, what grade she was in, and what things she liked to do. She was very nice and seemed genuinely interested. She said she knew Miranda's parents and had driven past the school before. Her daughter, Jennifer, was a sophomore at Pete's Grove High School. As more kids started pouring into the gym Teri told her it was nice to meet her and then turned her attention to the other kids.

Miranda and Susan joined in with a group of kids who were playing a game of spoons on the floor. Miranda loved this game because it didn't take any brain power but was immensely fun and chaotic.

Each person had a hand of four cards and they were they were each being constantly handed a card but they could only keep four cards in their hand at any time. Once someone got four of a kind they would slyly reach down and grab a spoon. From that point on anyone could grab a spoon. There was one less spoon in the middle than there were people playing so the last one that didn't notice all the spoons had been taken was the loser. It was a really fast paced game if there were a lot of people and sometimes Miranda didn't even bother watching the cards she would just keep passing cards along and watch the pile of spoons to see if anyone was sneaking one.

Miranda thought about her mom, she would probably come up with some kind of deep philosophical meaning behind this strategy about life passing quickly and the importance of paying attention to what was most important to you. Miranda thought about that, "What is the most important thing to me?" Right now she guessed it was friendship and it was great to be able to hang out with a group of friends her age and laugh. For a brief moment she thought about Emily. It must be really hard for her to be a senior and know she is missing out on all these great activities. Once again she wondered if there was anything she could do for her.

After a while the group came together in the middle of the gym and had a short devotional. Their youth group leader, Perry Been, led a prayer and included Emily's recovery in it. He then talked to them about the football game and how it related to life. That sometimes you were in the game, sometimes you were on the sidelines cheering, sometimes you were in the marching band and sometimes you were selling pickles and hot dogs.

Each phase of your life was going to give you an opportunity to play different roles. Sometimes you might get hurt, or feel like a loser and sometimes you have to work really hard and sometimes things go well and you feel like a winner. The important thing about life is that you keep showing up and playing your role the best you could trusting that God could use you just where you were if you were willing to ask for help in knowing how.

After the talk they sang a few songs. Miranda didn't know all the songs but she liked to listen to the voices blending together. It felt soothing and hopeful.

After the devotional was over Susan and Miranda walked out to the parking lot where Miranda's mom was waiting for her. Miranda gave Susan a hug and they promised to see each other soon. Katura waved at Susan as Miranda opened the door of the car.

"Good to see you Susan, tell your mom hello for me." Katura called out pleasantly.

"I will tell her, good to see you too Mrs. Cockrum." Susan waved good bye as they pulled out of the parking lot.

"Did you have a good time Miranda?" her mom asked cheerfully.

"It was great. Pete's Grove won and we played spoons and ate a lot. So a fun night all around! I also found out that Josiah's step sister Emily goes to church here. They had a bulletin board with pictures of her on it." Miranda suspected that her mom knew about her crush on Josiah but she had never really come right out and told her. It wasn't that she didn't trust her mom with her feelings, but she also didn't feel comfortable talking with her about it.

"Oh, did they say how she is doing?" Katura questioned.

"I think she is doing a lot better. I don't know how much longer she will have to stay at the rehab place for physical therapy. The youth group here has been doing some fundraisers to help her parents with the expenses. I feel so sorry for her, it must be so boring for her to be stuck there and know she is missing out on so much of her senior year. I wish I knew something I could do to help her." Miranda replied.

Katura smiled at her, "Miranda, you are a smart girl, if you think about it and you are meant to do something, I'm sure you will figure it out."

Miranda smiled back at her mom. Her mom's gentle confidence was always encouraging to her. Maybe she could find a way to help Emily.

She thought about it some more that night as she was reading part of her book about Martin Luther King, Jr. before she went to sleep. She was reading letters from a Birmingham Jail from April

16, 1963, she liked the quote, "I can't sit idly by in Atlanta and not be concerned about what happens in Birmingham. Injustice anywhere is a threat to justice everywhere. We are caught in an inescapable network of mutuality, tied in a single garment of destiny. Whatever affects one directly, affects all indirectly."

Emily was in a hospital bed not a jail cell, and the injustice of losing her senior year to take time to recover was certainly not the same as what Martin Luther King, Jr. had been talking about, but Miranda did somehow feel connected to her, tied in a single garment of mutuality. She thought about this as put the book on her bedside table and turned off the lamp.

I looked around and as far as I could see there was sand. It was hot and I didn't know where I was going or how far I would have to travel to get there. In the distance I could see a small figure. I walked towards her, it was a little girl, she was thirsty and hurt. I reached into my backpack and gave her some water. Then I asked her how long she had been there. The little girl shrugged her shoulders. How could someone have just abandoned her here I wondered. I decided to walk to a nearby dune to see if I could see further to see if there was anyone who could help us. I was nearly to the top of the dune when my foot tripped on something and I went stumbling back down. I sat at the bottom of the dune for a moment then climbed back again to where I had tripped. There sticking out of the sand was an enormous egg. It had cracked a bit and inside was a baby dragon with emerald green eyes. It hobbled out and started growing then it bent low before me. I climbed on its back and we flew back to the girl. I picked her up gently and we both sat on the back of the dragon. Then the dragon soared high into the air flying far from the sandy desert.

Miranda woke up, her throat was dry and her body felt like she had been in a desert. This wasn't a good sign. She went down the hall and got a drink of water and then collapsed back into bed. In the morning her mom came into wake her, took one look at her and said, "You don't look good Miranda."

Miranda's throat felt like it was on fire. Her mom got a thermometer and took her temperature. Yuck. Why did she have to get sick on a Saturday? Not fun. Not fun at all! Katura made an appointment for her at the local convenient care clinic. Wonderful, now not only was she sick but she would have to get up and go out into public looking sick.

The doctor declared, "Tonsillitis" and gave her mom a prescription for an antibiotic and encouraged Miranda to get lots of sleep. No problem there Miranda thought.

Miranda slept through the afternoon. When she woke up she saw that Candy had painted her a get well card. It had pink hearts and a big bowl of ice cream on it. That looked good. She got up and wandered downstairs where Candy and her mom were preparing dinner. They were making vegetable soup and Candy was putting out the ingredients her mom had told her to get. There was rice in the rice maker. Miranda told Candy thanks for the card.

"You're welcome, I just wanted to try and make you feel better. We got ice cream for you for dessert tonight."

"Aww…thanks!"

Miranda went up to her room and got her guitar. When she got back to the kitchen Candy was sitting on a stool drawing in her sketchbook. Miranda pulled out a stool next to her and starting playing the song that Meghan had taught her when she had visited. Miranda was trying to get better at it so she could play for Meghan if came back with Matthew at Christmas. After a while she looked up and noticed that Candy had started a new drawing. This one was of an airplane and there was a girl that looked a lot like Meghan at one of the windows of the airplane waving to a boy that looked a lot like Matthew on the ground. They both looked sad. Miranda wondered what Candy thought about Matthew and Meghan's relationship. She didn't say anything though. She turned back to her guitar and started working on a new song. It was a Green Day song that she had watched a YouTube video of to learn how to play. It was pretty simple but she wasn't quite sure how well she was doing until she heard her sister softly singing to herself, "I hope you have the time of your life..." Miranda looked up and grinned at her. She loved her sister.

That was when an idea formed in her head. Maybe she could go to see Emily and play some songs for her. She wasn't that great but she wasn't that bad either, and maybe Emily would like to have some company. Miranda looked up at her mom at the stove stirring the vegetable soup.

"Mom, do you think Josiah's sister would like it if I took my guitar and went to play for her sometime?"

"I don't know. It sounds like a great idea but maybe you could call and ask first before you went so you can find out if she feels up to having visitors and when would be a good time. Of course you are also going to have to wait until you are completely well yourself."

Miranda smiled, Christmas vacation was coming up, maybe she could go visit Emily and play for her then.

CHAPTER 13...Christmas

Miranda couldn't believe that Christmas vacation was almost over. Her family had decided to go to Gatlinburg for a few days to go skiing. They had rented a house and invited Meghan to come with them. Miranda could tell that Matthew and Meghan's feelings for one another were getting stronger with time. He had given her a silver necklace with a musical note on it for Christmas. She had knit him a warm muffler and hat in a rich green color that matched his eyes. Miranda liked the way Meghan seemed to have a calming effect on Matthew. He seemed happy most of the time, or maybe he was just maturing.

It was nice to be in a different place. Miranda and Candy were sitting out on the porch of the rented house when their dad came out with a bag of Doritos and sat next to them. Candy reached for some chips and Miranda noticed the picture of a smiling girl on the back of the bag. She tilted the bag toward her so she could read about 22 year old Maggie Doyne who was a winner of the Dorito: Do Something award. The young girl had gone back packing in Asia and saw the need for an orphanage in Nepal and used her own savings to build one. That was amazing. Miranda showed it to her dad. He was equally impressed. They started talking about the type of courage it must have taken for a 22 year old girl to attempt such a big feat. Miranda looked out at the newly fallen snow. It made everything look so fresh and new like anything was possible. Miranda thought about her own future, she considered what type of adventures she might have. What type of courage would she need in order to rise up for the challenges ahead? In school they were focusing on the idea of "The Heroic Journey" and Miranda knew that whatever she did in her life she didn't want to live a small life. She wanted to do things that would make the world a better place. She wanted to travel and meet all kinds of people, and she wanted to find ways to help people where ever she was.

CHAPTER 14...The National Civil Rights Museum

As much as she liked being on vacation Miranda was actually ready to go back to school. It was time for another immersion week and her class was going to The National Civil Rights Museum in Memphis. They were even going to be staying in a hotel in Memphis that had ducks that lived in the hotel. Miranda had never been to the museum even though Memphis wasn't that far away. The museum was housed in what was once The Lorraine Motel, the place where Martin Luther King, Jr. was assassinated on April 4, 1968.

She walked through the museum with Sheneca and Charlie by her side. They took turns reading about some of the different events that happened in the struggle for civil rights for African Americans. When they got to the bus that represented the famous Montgomery bus boycott that Rosa Parks began by refusing to give up her seat and move to the back of the bus just because she was African American, Miranda remembered one of the things Miss Walker had told them was that one of the reasons that it became such a big deal when Rosa did this was because she was a woman that was known in her community for having a high moral character. People respected her and respected what she did. Miranda had thought about that a lot, about how important having a strong moral compass seemed to be in doing big things in the world. As the girls entered the bus they got a surprise when a loud voice boomed through the bus telling them to move to the back.

Miranda thought about the lunch sit-ins that started in North Carolina. Both black and white students had protested together in order to change the laws so restaurants across the nation would give equal service to customers regardless of their race. When she passed the exhibit of the jail cell she thought about how much courage it must have taken for Martin Luther King, Jr. to make the decision to choose non-violent means of protesting, even when he knew it would land him in jail. Miss Walker reminded them often that peace is not the easy path, in fact it is frequently the most challenging.

When they reached the exhibit of the garbage workers and the hotel room when the assassination occurred Miranda looked at Sheneca out of the corner of her eye and wondered what going through this museum must feel like for her since her grandparents had played an active part in the protest. Miranda was glad to be Sheneca's friend and glad that the Walking In One Another's Shoes activity had drawn them closer together.

As the girls were waiting for everyone to get back together Miranda read the information on an exhibit about how Martin Luther King, Jr. had been highly influenced by Mahatma Gandhi's beliefs about the best way to transform society was through non-violent means that encouraged people to work together for civil rights for everyone. Miranda had always liked the Gandhi quote, "Be the change you want to see in the world."

After going to the National Civil Rights Museum Miss Walker took them to see the graduate building for the Memphis College of Art. It was a beautiful tall building with a glass window going all the way up the corner of the building. The window showcased a big red staircase. When you stood on the staircase you could look outside and see the green trolley cars passing by. Miss Walker was friends with Ben, one of the teachers at the graduate center and he showed the class around the building and even took a group picture of them on the red staircase. It was interesting seeing some of the art work of the students. One of the pieces was a sculpture done with different parts of a piano. The artist, William Smith, told the students that the piece represented people like Martin Luther King, Jr. who had important things to say and how even though their lives and voices seemed to have been torn apart, in reality they just went on in different forms like the piano was doing. Now those voices that speak for equality and justice continue on through students who have friendships that at one point would never have been allowed to have flourished in our country. Miranda couldn't help thinking about that as she stood next to Sheneca and watched Hannah and Caroline giggling together as they all stood together on the red stairs waiting to have their picture taken. A feeling of gratitude flowed over her as she thought about all the people who had sacrificed so much so she could be standing on this staircase today with her friends.

Leaving the graduate center the group decided it was time to eat. Walking down the street they found several places to eat and decided to go to a small café. As they ate their lunches Miranda noticed that Miss Walker and one of the chaperons, Sheneca's dad, were sitting together. He was telling her about the part Sheneca's grandparents had played in the protests. Miss Walker was really interested in what he was telling her and Miranda noticed her teacher's smile seemed even brighter than usual.

CHAPTER 15…Miranda's Great Idea

The days seemed to melt into one another like the occasional snowmen Candy and Miranda made during their frequent snow days. Miranda loved the miracle of snow days, the unexpected joy of waking up to discover the whole world had turned into a glistening wonderland as they slept. Even though Miranda missed hanging out with her friends at school, she and Candy made the best of the snowy days by having snowball fights and drinking hot chocolate by the fireplace. They got out the monopoly board and played several games to pass the time. She also spent time perfecting some new songs on the guitar. She had been going with Josiah to see Emily at the rehabilitation center and playing for her at least once a week when the weather was good.

The first time she had gone during Christmas break, she had felt really shy and awkward but Emily had such a cheerful personality that Miranda soon felt she was the one being encouraged. She had played a few songs for her and then they just started talking. Emily told her that Josiah had talked about her before. Josiah seemed to blush which made Miranda wonder what he had said, and hoped it was good.

There were cards and balloons all over the room. Miranda told Emily about seeing pictures of her hiking that were on the bulletin board at the church she had gone to with Susan. Emily had smiled, "Yes, I love to hike, and I look forward to getting out of here so I can do it again." Her doctors had told her that her therapy was going really well and she should be able to leave in a few weeks. Emily was excited about going back to school and finishing up her senior year. She wasn't going to be able to go on the mission trip and that had made her sad but she felt sure that something else important was going to come along that she could do. Miranda admired her positive attitude. It reminded her of a book she had read called, *Who Moved My Cheese?* The book was about mice in a maze that had to continually readjust to finding where their cheese had been moved to or what things they would have to do to get their cheese. The idea behind the book was that life is not static. It changes a lot and you can either stay where you are and be depressed because you don't like the changes or consider it a challenging adventure and keep going boldly on doing whatever you have in front of you to do next. Emily was obviously not going to waste time feeling sorry for herself.

One day after their visit Miranda had an idea about how to raise money to help Emily. She would have to talk to her parents and Matthew about it first, but the more she thought about the plan, the more excited she got about it. In fact she was so excited about it she wasn't really paying attention when she realized Josiah had reached for her hand as they were walking out of the door. It seemed so natural and so completely amazing all at the same time. When they got to the edge of the road where his mom was waiting in her green jeep to take them home their hands dropped to get into the car. Josiah opened the front door of the jeep to let her in and took her guitar and set it on the seat beside him. Josiah's mom had the radio set to an upbeat soft rock station and the music seemed to distract her from noticing the identical goofy grins that seemed to have grown on both Miranda and Josiah's face. When the car reached her house

Miranda thanked his mom for driving them and got out of the car. Josiah got out and carried her guitar for her to her front porch. As she looked up into his smiling face she wondered what to say but thankfully he saved the day by reaching down and just squeezing her hand. He looked down at her and said, "Thanks for caring about Emily, it means a lot to me." Miranda smiled, squeezed his hand back, and just said, "Your welcome. She is wonderful. I'm glad I'm getting to know both of you better."

Miranda went into the house to find her mom to share her great idea but first she felt the need to just breathe and think about what had just happened. Josiah had held her hand. What did that mean? She did a twirl in the hallway and then rushed off to find her mom.

Miranda's mom thought her idea to ask Matthew and his band to give a concert and have the donations go to help Emily's family with the hospital bills was a great idea. Emily quickly called Matthew. Her brother said he would have to talk to the other band members but he was definitely willing to do it.

In a few hours Matthew called her back and told her that the only time they all had free for the concert would be the weekend of Valentine's Day. That was only two weeks away. That didn't give her much time to organize but hopefully she could recruit some friends to help her out. During the sharing time of community meeting the next day Miranda revealed her idea and asked for help. She had already called her friend Susan and Susan had gotten permission to use the church gym for the concert. Everyone was very excited about the idea and agreed to stay after school and help make flyers and then pass them out in town. Some of the girls volunteered to come up with decorations for the gym. They decided they would have a concessions stand and buy some Jones sodas and chips to sell to raise even more money. They knew because of the short notice a lot of people might not be able to come but they decided to hope for the best and Sheneca agreed to create an events page on Facebook so they could get an idea of how many people would be coming. It amazed Miranda how quickly everything seem to be coming together. She had called Josiah the night before to ask what he thought of the idea and he had seemed really touched that Matthew would be willing to do this for Emily. As she was explaining the idea to the class she couldn't help wondering again how he felt about it. She felt sure he was appreciative but since he hadn't openly talked to the class about what happened, it felt like she needed to be careful about how she said things. Apparently she did o.k. though because when she glanced his way at the end the conversation he gave her a reassuring smile that told her the idea had been exactly the right choice.

As the day got underway though Miranda noticed that she was getting funny looks from her new group leader, Stephanie. It took Miranda awhile to figure it out but then she finally realized that Stephanie had concluded that Miranda had developed a closer relationship with Josiah then most people in the class had guessed. It seemed Stephanie was not excited about this turn of events. It made Miranda realize that being in her group this cycle might become a little bit tricky, especially when Stephanie made a snide comment about "how Miranda's outside activities had better not interfere with the group work they had to get done."

In a few weeks the group was going to be presenting a wax museum of famous Nobel Peace Prize winners. Each group also had to do special activities in preparation for the day. Miranda was in the chocolate group and they were responsible for creating a brochure for the event that listed all the winners the students were portraying and a short summary about how each winner contributed to peace. At first Stephanie told Miranda to start typing the information for their group but when she saw the green group was at the computers, and there was an open computer next to Josiah, Stephanie changed her mind and said she would do it. She wanted Miranda to spend time interviewing other classmates to get the information they wanted on the brochure.

As Miranda moved to interview some of the people in the red group she heard Stephanie loudly saying to Josiah, "I'm so glad we are going to be able to do something to help out Emily. Can you tell me more about her?"

Miranda rolled her eyes and sat down next to Carolina to ask for her information. Carolina had already written the information down so Miranda just had to sit there and copy it. She couldn't help glancing up to see how Josiah was responding to Stephanie. Since he spoke much quieter than Stephanie she couldn't hear his response but she could tell he seemed more interested in working on his group's power point than talking with Stephanie. Miranda couldn't help smiling to herself.

Carolina's winner was Wangari Maathai, the Nobel Peace Prize winner from 2004. She was the first East and Central African woman to earn her PhD and she was the founder of the Green Belt Movement, an organization that provides sustenance and income to people living in Kenya through the planting of trees. They also work to raise awareness about women's rights, civic empowerment, and environmental issues in Africa.

As Miranda moved through the room collecting information about the different Nobel Peace Prize winners she was struck by how different their lives were and how many different things they had done that had led to them winning the prize. She also saw once again the sacrifices and hardships some of them had endured because of their beliefs about the importance of peace. She was struck with how sad it was that Aung San Suu Kyi, the winner of the 1991 prize had been held under house arrest for many years by her government and had not been allowed to be with her husband when he died. Ling May had a picture of Aung San Suu Kyi and Miranda was taken aback by how young and beautiful she looked. Somehow in her mind she always associated people who won the prize as being really old and wrinkled like you had to be ancient to really understand the importance of peace, so it was a paradigm shift to think of someone that looked so youthful winning it.

Kelton was doing the organization, Amnesty International. The winner of the 1977 prize, the goals of the organization are to work for the protection of rights of prisoners of conscience. Kelton said he chose it because it reminded him of the jail cell they had seen when they went on the field trip to the National Civil Rights Museum. He was planning on using strips of white cloth around his wrists and put make up on his face to look like he had been beaten when he dressed up for the wax museum. He seemed really excited about this.

Miranda moved through the room collecting information and talking with different people about both the wax museum and about the concert. It was fun to hear different people's ideas and suggestions. The girls were especially excited about hearing the band play. Carolina giggled when Hannah boldly stated, "Let's face it Miranda, your brother is hot!" Miranda didn't know what to say to that so she just shook her head and grinned at them both then moved on to interview her next person.

CHAPTER 16...The Concert

As Miranda looked around the gym she was really impressed with how all their hard work had come together. There was a great crowd of both students from Peaceful Farm and from the local public schools. Susan had been the perfect person to get the news out and had even put a PSA about the concert out on the local radio station. There were even a lot of parents who came. Miranda noticed that Sheneca's dad was standing next to Miss Walker. They both seemed to be enjoying the band and talking a lot.

Miranda, Susan, and Charlie were helping with the concessions. The Green Eyed Boys had actually donated some special bottles of Jones Soda with pictures of the band on it to commemorate the event. Miranda noticed that both Carolina and Hannah bought one.

The most wonderful part about the concert though was when Matthew announced that they had a special guest who was at the concert that night. That was when Josiah appeared from a side door wheeling in Emily in a wheel chair that a big balloon tied on it that said, "Thank You!" The crowd went wild! Everyone was really happy to see her, especially her friends from the church. Then the band sang a song that Matthew had written just for the concert. He had played it for Miranda over the phone. It was about Emily and the importance of continuing to put one foot in front of another even when life didn't turn out the way you expected. Emily was grinning and crying at the same time when she heard it.

After the concert Josiah's dad and step-mother and Emily came up to tell Miranda how much they appreciated all she had done to help Emily. Miranda felt humbled because it had been such a group effort and so much fun that she didn't feel like she really deserved any thanks. She was happy that Emily had been able to come to the concert and gave her a big hug. She blushed when Emily whispered in her ear, "I'm so glad Josiah has such a sweet girlfriend!" Then winked at her.

Josiah's mom was going to pick him up later because he had promised to stay and help clean up. Miranda wanted to ask him about what Emily had said but decided that saying something might spoil the hopeful moment. Miranda started stacking chairs while Josiah helped the band pack up their equipment. When they were both finished Miranda went up to where her parents were talking with Sheneca's dad and Miss Walker. Miranda told them she was going to wait outside with Josiah for his mom to come pick him up. As they walked out they looked up at the stars that seemed close enough to reach out and pluck from the sky. Josiah just looked at her and grinned. He reached for her hand and said, "I really want to thank you for everything you did, it was all so spectacular. You have a good heart Miranda. Then he reached into his coat pocket and pulled out a small red package. She almost hated to let go of his hand to accept the gift. She could tell her own hands were shaking as she pulled a small gold heart necklace out of the box. Josiah took the necklace from her and leaned towards her to fasten it around her neck. Miranda was pretty sure he could probably hear how fast her heart was beating when he quietly whispered, "Miranda, will you be my Valentine?" It felt like a moment from a movie…until suddenly something very cold and wet side swiped both of them.

Miranda could hear Jeffrey's buoyant laughter at his well-timed snow ball.

Josiah and Miranda looked at each other and both started laughing as they reached down to pack up snowballs to return the favor. A group of other students including Sheneca and Toby had just walked out of the building and joined them in what turned out to be a fantastic snowball fight.

CHAPTER 17…Changes

As the fourth cycle steadily marched on the students got ready for the Nobel Peace Prize wax museum and for their upcoming standardized testing. Miranda was glad that Miss Walker seemed more interested in the preparations for the wax museum than the testing. Susan had told her that the teachers at their school had them doing tons of practice tests and were all stressed out and grouchy. Miranda wondered how any of the students could learn anything in that kind of environment. On the contrast Miss Walker seemed happier than she had ever seen her. Almost as if she had a special secret that was tugging the corners of her mouth in a permanent upward position.

This was also the two weeks of the cycle when the class was working on science, or natural world as they called it. The topic this cycle was machines and electricity. Their group had to work together to create a machine using the six simple machines that would then be used to make a compound machine that would transfer a small piece of paper into a cup. Miranda was glad they had Dinah in their group because she really got into making the machine. Miranda had a feeling their group was going to have the best machine. Which was good because knowing that Dinah was focusing the most on the machine left Miranda time to really work on her Nobel Prize speech for the wax museum. Her winner was Jody Williams, the 1997 winner for her efforts to ban landmines through the International Campaign to Ban Landmines. Sitting at the computers Miranda clicked on http://www.nobelwomensinitiative.org and started

writing the information it gave about Jody
Williams's thoughts about peace:
"An outspoken peace activist who struggles to
reclaim the real meaning of peace-a concept which
goes far beyond the absence of armed conflict and
is defined by human security, not national security.
Williams believes that working for peace is not for
the faint of heart. It requires dogged persistence
and a commitment to sustainable peace, built on
sustainable development, environmental justice and
security, and meeting the basic needs of the
majority of people on our planet."

Miranda enjoyed reading about Williams,
she seemed so personable and real. Reading about
the land mines gave Miranda the chills though, war
was bad enough, but to realize that landmines
caused innocent civilians to lose their lives years
after wars were over was a horrendous thought. It
made her really angry. All the resources that war
cost could be used for uplifting people instead of
tearing them down.

One of the quotes she ran across that was
attributed to Jody Williams was in a thesis paper
written by a Montessori teacher. The quote said, "If
each one of us or even just a handful found a way to
make the world a better place, can you imagine the
difference we would make?"

This quote made Miranda realize she could
either get angry at war or get busy for peace. If
only she could figure out what her way to make the
world a better place was. It was true that she
couldn't do everything, but that shouldn't stop her
from doing the things she could.

After school Miranda went to see Mrs.
Love. She asked her mentor what she thought about
how she could find her "peace mission". Mrs. Love

encouraged her to begin with learning how to approach each moment of her life with a desire to include peace as a top priority, to realize that in every situation you could choose peace. Once she got into the habit of always choosing what would bring her spirit the most peace the path would become clearer. She warned her that peace did not mean she would never struggle with problems, it only meant finding a way to solve the conflict with creativity and joy in a way that would build up herself and the people around her instead of tearing them down. She said you had to listen your heart and sometimes that would mean confronting someone when your own heart felt troubled, but to always value the relationship and to be kind when confronting.

During reflection time the next day Miranda thought about the theme for their current cycle, "Changes". Miranda thought about what that meant, about the changes that were happening in her life in that moment. There was the growing friendship between her and Josiah, Emily's recovery, the things she was learning academically, and the things she was learning about peace. There were also changes for the future that she was starting to think about like going to the public high school and then eventually choosing a college and a career. It was a lot to think about, but she decided she should follow Mrs. Love's advice and trust that all she had to really concentrate on was the decisions to be made right in front of her and how to feel peace about those decisions.

Sometimes though, it was interesting to let her thoughts meander and consider how the things she was doing now might inform the future. For instance she had discovered she really enjoyed working with Jeffrey, especially helping him with reading. For Christmas she had used the garage band feature on the school computer to record herself reading some books to him then given him the books to read along with. He had been really excited about it and Sheneca had told her that she often heard him listening to the books at night time when he was going to bed. He especially seemed to like a children's book by Dan Millman book, *The Way of The Peaceful Warrior*. It was about a boy who was being bullied and how a new friend, "Socrates" helped him learn how to fight, and how to be at peace.

Working with Jeffrey made her think that she might enjoy teaching someday, or at least working with kids in some way. She had even chosen to do her internship for the Heroic Journey at the local public library. The local director of the library, Ms. Nancy Canada had been there as long as she could remember. Miranda had so many memories of going to Story Time when she was little, Ms. Nancy always brought the most delicious snacks and would plan fun programs. One program was about snakes, it was the first time Miranda had ever touched a snake. A park ranger came to story time and brought a small snake with him for the kids to learn about. Before that Miranda had only been interested in reading fiction stories, but the park ranger had read them real stories about snakes and it had made her want to read and learn more about them. She had been so surprised that snakes were not at all slimy but felt very smooth and cool to her touch.

CHAPTER 18...Balance

It felt like the calendar had been tilted and all the days had floated away like the tufts of the dandelions that Candy loved to blow into the vast spring afternoons. The year was almost over. Miranda was bent over the wooden power shield that she had carefully decoupaged with pictures of the year. She smiled as she saw one of her and Josiah covered in mud from their time working on the straw bale house. That seemed so long ago but she could still remember how honored she had been when he had shared with her his feelings about Emily.

There was a picture of Emily and Matthew from the concert and a picture of all her classmates together on the day of the Wax museum. The newest additions included a picture of her playing her guitar during the fundraiser for World Water Day. It had been a part of her heroic journey challenge to write and perform a song for the day. She had been really nervous but it made her feel really proud when everyone clapped and put money in her guitar case to donate to help Amman Imman build a well in Africa. Mrs. Love had been right about just doing the next thing she could for peace over and over, trusting those little steps would make a difference.

The power shield was going to be a visual to use when Miranda talked to the Council of Elders about her year and what she had learned from it. The Council of Elders was made up of members of the community that were people that Miss Walker respected and chose as wise role models. They would listen to each of the students tell about their year and then give them advice and feedback about the things they had told them.

Miss Walker was going to let them practice in class sharing their shields and their stories so they wouldn't be so nervous talking with the Council of Elders but Miranda almost wondered if sharing with the class didn't make her more nervous. She wondered if she should practice in front of her mirror or just wing it. Just then Candy knocked on her door, "Whatcha doing?"

Miranda gave her a big smile and said, "Come here and I'll show you."

Starting with the color scheme which was in shades of purple Miranda started explaining about the shield and the different things that had happened during the year that she felt had changed her or impacted her in some way. She paused when she got to the picture of her and Josiah.

"You really like him don't you?" Candy said in a quiet voice.

"Yes, he has been a good friend to me this year and a lot of the things that happened that changed me had to do with him."

Candy looked at her as if she was peering into her soul. "You are going to miss him next year aren't you?"

Miranda gave her a sad smile, "Yep."

Candy reached up and gave her a hug. "But you will still have me, and I will still have you for at least one more year."

Candy's statement surprised Miranda, she hadn't really thought about how going to high school would mean leaving her little sister behind. She remembered what it felt like when Matthew left and went to public school. She would still see him in the afternoons and evenings but it had been sort of sad and lonely not to go to his locker and have treats that he saved just for her. Then it seemed like right after that he was gone for college. She would have to find a way to help Candy not feel lonely when she left, maybe she could slip notes into her back pack or something for her to read during the school day.

"That is right, and we can do lots of fun things next year to make it special and before you know it you will be the one making a shield and going before the Council of Elders. Do you want to help me attach the ribbon to the back so it can hang up?"

"Sure." Candy chose an orange ribbon to go on the back. Miranda had told her that colors are very significant that they have meanings attached to them. Candy had liked that because she loved bright colors. Purple was the color Miranda had chosen for the shield because it was the color of transformation and it reminded her of the Irises blooming outside her window. They were so tall and looked so elegant.

It made her think of how she was growing, she wasn't where she was going to be, but she had come a long way from where it felt like she had started the year. The orange ribbon made her think of happy things, energy and sunlight, summer fun about to happen after such a big year of changes.

The biggest event of the summer was going to be another wedding at the school. Miranda grinned as she remembered Sheneca's announcement during community meeting that she would have a new mom soon. Everyone was shocked and delighted when they found out that it was going to be their teacher, Miss Walker! Apparently Miss Walker and Mr. Jones had realized how much they had in common during school events and late nights chatting away on Facebook. Sheneca said that the romance had been a surprise to her, but that her dad was really happy and they had been doing activities together as a family, and Miss Walker had been really good for Jeffrey. The wedding was going to be in mid-June. Sheneca was going to be a bridesmaid and had been looking through magazines to figure out how to fix her hair for the occasion. Miranda was really glad that the Heroic Journey and the Walking in one Another's Shoes activity had brought her and Sheneca closer. Miss Walker was going to be such a great mom for her.

As she thought about the wedding she also thought about Jeffrey and how close they had also grown over the year. She had never expected that. He still liked to tease, but now it seemed more like in a fun way not in a bratty way. Maybe her dad had been right about some people needing more love than others.

Talking about her shield with Candy had made her feel more comfortable with talking to the Council of Elders. Now she felt like she was sharing good memories and that was always fun to do. She was also going to be singing the song for them that she had performed on the day of the fundraiser. The words ran through her mind:

> Little child, little child.
> So far away from my world.
> Without a drop of water in sight how will
> you sleep tonight?
> Little child, little child
> It may be up to me to make it right.

So I give you what I've got and hope it is
enough.
I give you my song and hope others will
sing along.
That they will understand that by giving a
helping hand they could forever change
your land.
Their dollar or dime today, could keep
death from taking your life away.
Little child, little child.
So far from my world, yet close to my
heart.
I can't do everything, but I can do my part.

CHAPTER 19...The Council of Elders

Miranda stood nervously outside the door of the classroom that had been set aside for the interviews with the Council of Elders. Charlie had been right before her and had come out with a big smile on her face and given her a hug, "It will be o.k. they are really very nice."

As Miranda walked in the room she could see the shields of the other students that had already been before the council. They were all so creative and different. Ling May had made hers in the shape of a ballet shoe, Christopher had made his in the form of a chess board and Steven had used an old tennis racquet to create his shield. Some people had used photos, drawings, or magazine pictures on their boards, but you could tell everyone had spent a lot of time on them.

There were six members of the Council of Elders, three women and three men. Miranda crossed the room and shook hands with each of them and introduced herself. She recognized one of the women as the lady that had served her punch at Susan's church the night of the fifth quarter. The woman smiled and told her it was good to see her again.

They asked her to share her shield and tell them about her year. Miranda realized her voice was shaky but as she got started she got excited about sharing her memories of the year. They asked her questions as she went along. They were really interested in how she organized the concert for Emily. Miranda explained that it had been a big endeavor but it had felt like something she was meant to do because it all came together so easily with everyone's help. She had the original thought but so many other people had added their own talents to help make it a success.

She got to a quote she had written, "You must adapt to new situations to avoid getting ulcers in life: if you fall into a mud puddle you should check your pockets for fish." The quote had made her think about Emily and Josiah, about how Emily's accident had changed so much of her life and plans. Miranda had been impressed with how Emily had made the best of it and was finding new ways to reach out. Instead of going to another country to do mission work Emily had decided to spend the summer tutoring local students that had come to America and had limited English skills. Emily was excited about it and had even recruited Josiah to help with it.

There was a picture of Mrs. Love and Miranda holding baby Zoe. Miranda told the council about how Mrs. Love had been her mentor for the year and some of the things they had done together. Miranda explained how both having a mentor and being a mentor to Jeffrey had made her realize how important it was to make friends with people that were different ages in order to always be learning something and to be passing it on. She even confessed with a blush how much she had always dreaded the idea of being around Jeffrey but this year he had come to mean a lot to her.

There was a picture of her at story time talking to some of the kids and sharing the peanut butter balls she had brought for snack. One of the men on the council, Mr. Peterson, was the president of the Friends of the Library and he told her that if she kept volunteering it might eventually work into a summer or afterschool job for her when she got into high school. Miranda liked that idea.

After sharing her stories Miranda told about the challenges she had chosen for the journey. For an academic challenge she had memorized several poems including one by Yeats that was written in metrical lines of verse called hexameters. The poem was titled, "The Lake Isle of Innisfree". She had discovered it when she was studying Ireland. Mrs. Walker had pointed out how poetry and math are often interlinked because poems follow rhythms and beats. Mrs. Walker also explained that the lyrics of music are really just other examples of poetry. Seeing the connection had helped her like language more as a subject.

For a physical challenge Miranda had started running in the mornings and had run a mile every day for the past month. She felt like she was more physically fit and was thinking that if she kept it up she might even go out for track when she got into high school.

The last thing that she did was play the song she had written as her personal challenge. She told them about the fundraiser and that she had raised $200 for it on her own. They liked the song and told her she should continue to look for ways to use her music to help others because it seemed like it was a path that was open for her.

The members of the Council of Elders all shook her hand and wished her well in the future. Miranda smiled a big smile. She felt like she had done well expressing herself and telling about the year. Hearing their comments and feedback had been encouraging and empowering.

When the interview was over she joined the rest of the students that had finished their interviews. They were all in the peace garden writing in their reflection journals about their experience or sitting around talking in small groups. Miranda pulled out her journal and wrote a page and a half about what sharing the year with the Council had been like. Then she drew a sketch of her shield and some of the shields of the other students.

Finishing her reflection she looked up to see Josiah walking towards her. "How did it go?" he asked as he sat down on the bench next to her.

"It was good, really good. Not nearly as scary as I expected. I felt like they were interested in what I had to say and very supportive. I actually liked it once I got into it. How did your interview go?"

Josiah smiled at her and said, "It was good, like you said, I felt like they were very supportive. Hey, I was wondering since we chose the same physical challenge if you might like to go running with me some this summer?"

"That would be great. You are probably going to be so fast though you will be farther ahead than me. Are you going to mind waiting for me?" Miranda held her breath and wondered if he caught her double meaning.

"Yep. You are definitely worth the wait." He grinned and lightly punched her on the shoulder.

CHAPTER 20...Celebrations

The peace garden twinkled with white lights everywhere. Small tables with brightly colored table cloths were set up in front of the podium that the class had used every day for community meeting. White votive candles flickered in the spring breeze as Miss Walker introduced each student in the class and their mentor.

Each mentor gave a short speech to tell the gathered audience about the student they had been with all year and the changes they had seen from the student. Miranda walked slowly to the podium to stand next to Miss. Love. It felt weird standing there and hearing her mentor talk about her in front of everyone, but a good kind of weird, sort of a mix of a sense of pride and a sense of responsibility to continue on and do well to live up to all the kind things she was saying. As she looked out at the audience she saw so many people that she had been influenced by during the year. Emily was sitting next to Josiah and both of them were giving her a big smile.

After all the speeches had been given Diane Turner gave a speech for the class to thank Miss Walker for all the things she had done for the class during the year and then presented a small water fountain that the students had chipped in to buy for the peace garden in honor of her. Diane talked about the significance of the fountain that it represented the way life continues on, big and small drops splashing down from all our lives, blending into the lives of others. How the students would never forget this year and the things Miss Walker had taught them about academic, personal, and social things like the importance of sharing water with others regardless of their skin color or how far away they lived from us, and just like the many drops we were all a connected part of each other.

Miranda looked over to the table where Sheneca, Jeffrey and Mr. Jones were sitting. Mr. Jones was beaming. You could tell he was proud of his future bride and proud of his kids. It was beautiful to see how love had transformed his life...wuv, tru, wuv...

Looking back at her own table she looked at her brother Matthew with his arm casually draped around Meghan's shoulder. Meghan had gotten a job offer in New York and had decided to take it which meant she would be apart from Matthew while he finished his last bit of school. Matthew had told Miranda that he felt Meghan was the girl he was going to marry someday but it was good for her to have a chance to experience life on her own for a little bit more before they settled down. He said that love was patient and kind, and he knew letting her go was the patient and kind thing to do at this time in their lives. He also said he was thankful for Skype and that he planned to save up all he could so he could fly to New York a few times to see her during school breaks.

Candy sat between Matthew and their mom and dad. Miranda took out the shiny red camera she had gotten for her birthday and took a picture of everyone at the table. It was a great picture with all of them smiling and the purple table cloth sparkling under the lights. It had been a good year, Miranda had learned a lot but the most important lesson might have been to take time to stop and celebrate the journey. Sometimes you need a moment to check your map and compass, but then you need to continue on. The world needs all the heroes it can get.